Twelve Days
A Tale of Christmas

In the spirit of *A Christmas Carol*, D.P. Conway writes a compelling story that will inspire you at this and every Christmas.

Barbara Disanto is on top of the world in business and life. The people all around her, though, are suffering from her relentless drive to the top.

Just before Christmas, a mysterious message begins to haunt her, telling her she must do something, 'before it is too late.'

D1521941

Twelve Day
is part of
The Christmas Collection

D. P Conway has written four memorable stories to warm your hearts and your homes this Christmas season.

In the spirit of Charles Dickens, Conway brings you Twelve Days and The Ghost of Christmas to Come.
Following, with equal luster, are Starry Night and Nava.

Start with any of the four books, and you will find yourself quickly wanting to read all.

Twelve Days

A Tale of Christmas

by D. P. Conway

Part of

The Christmas Collection

Day Lights Publishing House, Inc.

Cleveland, Ohio

From Darkness to Light through the Power of Story

Dedications

For Marisa
Thank you for helping me to keep Christmas well.
Io Ti Amo Sempre.

For Patrick
Keep Leading the Way

For my biggest fans, my children,
Colleen, Bridget, Patrick, and Christopher.

And for my littlest fans,
my little Aubrey
and my little Avery.

For Bruna

The Story of the Writing of Twelve Days.

Long ago, Charles Dickens looked about London, England and realized that they were not keeping Christmas well. So, he set out to write a story that might change things. *A Christmas Carol* was born, and it did change everything. It would be said later that Dickens was the man who invented Christmas.

This past Christmas, I, too, looked around and noticed we were not keeping Christmas well. I could not help but feel the mad rush of families trying to fit it all in, to be here at this time, and there at that time, to be everywhere and through it all, be too rushed to even think about Christmas. It would all go on in a tiny window from 4:30 p.m. on Christmas Eve until Christmas night. By then, most of us would collapse with exhaustion, unfulfilled, thrilled—not for Christmas, but that the mad shopping season that began on Black Friday was finally through. I said to myself, "We are not keeping Christmas well."

At the very same time, I had a boss who was less than kind. He was not a bad person in any regard, but he was mad most of the time.

I thought to myself, "Hmmmm…. I have an idea."

And *Twelve Days* was born.

During this particular year, my wife and older son and I worked hard to keep Christmas well. We went to Mass each evening in beautiful churches so warmly decorated for Christmas. As I was writing this book, conscious of the phrase Dickens made famous, we often said, "We are keeping Christmas well."

I hope you enjoy this story, and I hope it will inspire you to not only keep Christmas well, but to also keep life well. God bless.

Now, sit back, and let me tell you a story.

D. P. Conway
June 11, 2021
In the Second Spring of the Covid 19 Pandemic

Christmas is Coming

Barbara DiSanto stormed out of her office and down the hall to the office of Jerry Tracek. Jerry was a junior associate in her advertising firm. He was much younger than Barbara, only 37 years old, of medium athletic build with silky dark brown hair. He had been with her for over two years now and was doing a very good job helping Barbara to bring new clients into the firm.

"Jerry!" she yelled as she approached the doorway and turned into his office, shaking a stack of papers in her hand.

Barbara was dressed flawlessly today, wearing a black Chiara Boni Jump Suit and matching Prada Leather Pumps. The ultra-expensive outfit made her 57-year-old body look like she was in her late 30s.

She abruptly stopped, throwing the stack of papers on the desk, demanding to know, "What is this?"

Jerry looked up; his eyes narrowed as kindly as they could without revealing his anger. He hated when she stormed in like a mad woman. He looked down at the pile of papers. "It is the proposal for Vocan."

Barbara exhaled loudly, brushed her neatly shaped, neck-length hair behind her ear, and lowered her chin. She glared and shouted sternly, "This is garbage, Jerry. I need you to redo this today *before* you go home. Do you understand?" Barbara's dark brown Italian eyes glared at him, and her dark red clenched lips did nothing to soften the look.

"What's wrong with it?" he asked in a surprised tone.

"You can't see what is wrong with it? If you can't see what is wrong with it, maybe it is time for me to get someone else in that chair."

Jerry swallowed. This was not the first time Barbara had threatened him.

She was a hard woman to work for. Not one of the nine people who worked in her company liked her. Still, she paid them well, and despite her critical, demeaning approach, she was right fairly often, which made her firm successful.

"I will look at it, but what exactly needs to be fixed?"

She stepped closer to the desk and leaned forward with a manufactured half-smile, "Jerry, I'll give you a hint. Go get the proposal I did for Smart Business and *read it*!"

"Okay," he replied quickly.

Barbara wheeled around and stormed back out without saying a word.

Jerry looked up at the time. It was already 1:30 p.m. on the day before Christmas Eve. He was running out of time.

He had promised his wife, Nina, that he would pick her up at 4:30 to go shopping at the mall. There was no way he would make it now. He grabbed his phone from his desk drawer and texted her.

"Hey honey, I'm sorry. The Wicked Witch of the North just flew in, and I may have to work late. I'll text you when I get out, but it might be late."

Jerry set his phone down, exasperated. He was getting tired of Barbara's antics: storming in unannounced with an angry tone, wagging her finger as if he were a child, glaring at him for no reason. These were but a few of her antics. He had hoped she might change, especially after some of the new clients he helped bring in; but now it seemed that nothing would ever change her. He turned his attention to the computer screen to check his email before going to the file room to get the Smart Business proposal.

His phone beeped. It was Nina. He sighed and opened her text.

"Why do you have to stay so late. Did you forget? After shopping, we were supposed to see my mom at the nursing home. Now we probably won't have time."

He hastily texted back.

"We will fit it in. I promise."

A text came back almost immediately.

"Jerry, the babysitter can't stay that long."

Jerry shook his head, slammed down his phone, cursing under his breath. Barbara did not need the work done today. The proposal was not due for two more weeks. She was just being a jerk. He got up and went to get the Smart Business proposal to figure out what she wanted.

* * * *

In her office on the 17th floor of Eaton Center, on Superior Avenue in Cleveland, Barbara had a view of the entire roof and grounds of St. John's Cathedral. It was located in the heart of downtown, right next door to her office.

The sight of the old Cathedral brought back memories of the old days. Her grandmother used to go to Mass there every day after work. She worked as the waitress at Boukair's Soda & Grill in the Hanna Building. Every day after work, rain or shine, she would make the 15-minute walk to the Cathedral. After the 5 p.m. Mass ended, she would take the bus to their home on Franklin Avenue, usually arriving for dinner by 6 p.m.

Barbara often wondered what possessed her grandmother to go to such lengths to attend Church. Growing up, her parents had been diligent about going to Mass on Sundays, but certainly not every day like her grandmother. Barbara never liked going at all, and once she went away to college, she stopped going altogether. In her mind, she was making an important generational step upward toward more modern thinking. Attending Mass was something the old folks did, in the old days, which were long since gone.

Barbara's two daughters went nearly every week, and Barbara did not understand why, as she certainly had not raised them to do so. She could only assume it was because of their husbands, neither of whom she felt were the cream of the crop in the enlightened thinking department.

Today was a particularly cloudy day, typical of Cleveland. But that was not what was troubling her. The words *before it's too late* wouldn't stop echoing in her mind. She had no idea where they came from.

She scanned the downtown skyline beyond the Cathedral for another moment, then turned back to face her desk. She had lots to do, including a dinner meeting with a prospect at 7 p.m. at the Hoffbrau House Restaurant. She was looking forward to the German dishes she rarely got to enjoy. Steve Garrity of Loktite Corp had an advertising budget of several million dollars a year. Barbara was sure she could do a better job than his current advertising agency was doing. She imagined the account would easily be worth hundreds of thousands in billing a year.

It was why she went to the trouble of having Martha, her personal assistant, buy her a new outfit with matching shoes and a matching purse two days earlier. She wanted to look perfect, and by the looks she had gotten walking into the building this morning, she had accomplished her goal.

The office phone rang.

"Yes?" Barbara said, hitting the intercom button and turning away from the view out the 17th-floor window wall to face her desk.

Kathy, her longtime secretary, announced, "I have Steve Garrity on the line."

Barbara sighed. *Was he calling to cancel?* No matter, she would face it head-on, like she did everything. Her father had taught her that long ago to face her problems head-on, without hesitation. He had also taught her to go and take what she wanted in life because no one was going to hand it to her.

She glared at the phone for a moment, gathering her resolve, then smiled and picked up the phone, "Hello, this is Barbara."

"Barbara, it's Steve Garrity. How are you today?"

"I'm good, Steve. I am looking forward to our dinner tonight."

"Yes, I am too. Are you ready for Christmas?"

Barbara rolled her eyes. She had no time for Christmas. She smiled, though, and replied, "Yes, as ready as I will ever be. But enough about Christmas, what can I do for you, Steve?"

"I've gone over your proposal."

"And?" Barbara said playfully, ready for the boom to drop, her mind already racing how she would counter it.

"And I love it. It is the most creative approach we have ever had presented to us. I wanted you to know, I am signing it right now."

"Oh, that's great, Steve. I am excited about the campaign."

"Me too. We can start getting into some of the nuances tonight at dinner."

"Great. I'll see you at 7."

"Excellent, Barbara. See you then."

Barbara hung up and gritted her teeth, thrusting her fists into the air. "Yes, I did it!"

She had been on a roll lately. Her firm, The Barbara DiSanto Company, had nearly doubled in size during the past two years. She still needed to get the final report from her lackluster accounting department, but she was fairly certain she had made over a million dollars in profit this year.

She turned to look out the window wall again, in the direction that overlooked the cathedral's roof. For some reason, she thought of her grandmother, slaving away at the counter of the tiny downtown restaurant. She had worked there for years, making barely enough money to help put food on the table. "Grandma," she said aloud to herself, "You would be very, very, proud of me."

Just then, her cell phone rang. It was her oldest daughter, Laura. "Mom, I got your message earlier, but we can't make it by 6 tomorrow."

"And why not?" Barbara replied, with her brow deeply furrowed.

"Because John wants to take the kids to Church."

Barbara's eyes narrowed further, "Laura, we are on a tight schedule tomorrow night. Leave Church early or go to Church another time."

"We will leave early, mom. I already told John we have to, but you know… it's crowded on Christmas Eve. It may take forever to get out of the parking lot."

"Listen to me carefully. I spent a lot of money on this dinner, *and* the gifts for you and the grandchildren. You guys do whatever you have to do, but dinner is at 6. I expect you to be there."

"Okay, then. What are we having again?" Laura asked, trying to deflect her mom's curtness.

"We are having lobster bisque soup, London Broil, and lobster tail. I also have Martha picking up chicken fingers and fries for the children at 5:30." Martha was Barbara's personal assistant and had been doing a myriad of things for her for over a year now.

"Mom, I will try. Hey, why don't you have one of us pick up the chicken? This way, Martha can get home to her family early for Christmas Eve."

"No," Barbara replied without hesitation. "It is already arranged, and that is what I pay her for."

"Yeah, I get it," Laura replied. "Oh, Mom. Uncle Steve called. His son Tom is in the hospital."

"With what?"

"He said it's some kind of blood disease."

Barbara commented, "He probably has AIDS."

There was silence.

"I thought you would want to know."

"I am too busy for that right now, Laura. Tom has made poor choices and now he is paying for them."

Again, there was silence.

Laura awkwardly broke it, saying, "Okay, we will see you tomorrow."

Barbara reminded her once more, "Don't be late," then hung up.

* * * *

The rest of the afternoon passed very slowly. Something was agitating Barbara, but she could not put her finger on it. It was as if there was some urgency for her to do something; though, what, she did not know. The feeling kept coming up, and she kept being drawn to look out at the sky over the cathedral roof.

At 4 p.m., she called Jerry Tracek's office and asked, "Jerry, what is happening?"

"What do you mean?"

"The proposal!!" she said in a stern tone.

"I am working on it!" he snapped.

"I want it done before you leave. Do you understand?"

"Yes, I understand."

She hung up, shaking her head. Sometimes she wished she could just do everything herself. It would save her a great deal of aggravation.

She wheeled around and returned to looking out the window. All around the cathedral, people were beginning to trickle into the various entrances. Evening Mass was approaching. Barbara had tried to go once, some ten years earlier. But there was a homeless black man who sat in the pew right behind her. To this day Barbara still remembered the stench around him. She wondered why the Church let people like that just walk in. It was certainly not good marketing.

Her office phone rang, jolting her out of her thoughts. Barbara hit the intercom button, "Yes?"

"Stan from accounting wants to meet with you."

"Tell him it will have to wait until after Christmas. I am busy and I have a meeting tonight."

"All right," replied her secretary.

Barbara hung up and smiled. She already knew what Stan wanted, and she was in no hurry to hand out bonuses, not at least until her year-end numbers were solidified.

She had learned this from her father, too. After years of failure in business, causing terrible arguments at home, he had finally started a successful plumbing supply store. He was a master in handling his employees, especially the ungrateful ones. Barbara loved his stories, of keeping his employees in line by yelling at them, or even firing them. She respected his ways and had made them her own. Had her siblings followed his advice, perhaps they would not be so poor.

* * * *

A moment later, the phone rang again. Barbara slammed her finger on the intercom. "What is it?" she asked in an indignant tone, the one she used when she wanted to intimidate her secretary.

"It's Stan again. He said it cannot wait."

Barbara's eyes vaulted to the ceiling as she shook her head. She closed her eyes, trying to calm the anger she felt welling up within her. She had disliked Stan and his work for at least six months now. After the year-end books were closed, she would contemplate getting rid of him. She shouted back at the intercom. "I'll decide if it can wait!"

Her secretary did not reply.

Barbara slammed her finger on the intercom button, disconnecting it. She glared out the window, then slammed her finger down again, reactivating the intercom, "tell him to come in now. And tell him it better be important!"

A few minutes later, Stan, a balding middle-aged accountant, whose rounded stomach perfectly complemented the rounded bald crown on his head, walked in.

"What is it, Stan?" she snapped with an authoritative, aloof voice.

"I have the healthcare numbers. There is a large increase."

"Now, two days before Christmas! How much of an increase?"

"Ummm, let's see here." Stan pushed his glasses higher up his nose and fumbled some papers, squinting. "Ummm, it says, 35 percent."

"Thirty-Five What!" she shouted, jumping out of her chair.

Stan raised his eyes, then furrowed his brow, staring back down at the number as if looking at them would somehow soften their impact.

Barbara slammed her fist on the desk, demanding, "When did you learn about this?"

"Last week, when I was out on quarantine with Covid."

"And you didn't think to call me?"

"I was in bed much of the week. I worked as much as I could. I had to push this off because you had me busy with other projects. I was supposed to address it Monday, but you blew up about the gas bill, and that tied me up the entire day."

"Why is it going up?" she snapped back at him.

"The agent told me because of Jennifer's cancer diagnosis."

Barbara gritted her teeth, "Do I have to pay for every person's problems?" She wheeled around to look out the window, feeling that strange urgency again, then asked, "How much is this going to cost a person who is on the family plan?"

"Six thousand more per year. But the employee has to pay most of that. We only pay the employee part. They pay for their family."

"Stan! In case you didn't remember, I pay all of it for my family. So… it is costing me $6,000 more personally!" She grimaced, throwing her hand in the air, then demanded, "What is the cost increase to the company?"

"It will cost the company $1,800 more a month. It's not too bad." He held his breath, waiting for the outburst.

Barbara stood up defiantly, saying, "That is over $20,000 a year, Stan! Plus, $6,000 more for me. That's $26,000 out of my pocket! Do you have $26,000 to throw around, Stan?"

Stan looked up and said firmly, "We are a growing company, Barbara. We have to expect things like this."

She raised her finger, "You listen to me. You have to find another policy for us. If it was your $26,000, you would be all over this. Or you know what, the hell with it, I will just cancel the insurance. Let everyone get their own insurance."

"Barbara, Jennifer has already started chemo treatments. You can't just...."

She interrupted, "I can do whatever I want, Stan. I didn't tell her to go and get cancer."

Stan felt stuck by her comment. He fumbled his thoughts for a moment, then said, "Well... but Barbara, you need to offer insurance to attract talent."

Barbara did not reply. She didn't need the 'talent' she had attracted, starting with Stan. "Oh, I suppose that is true," she said, her voice trailing, pretending what he said mattered. She then snapped, "But I don't care right now. Find a cheaper plan, or I will discontinue insurance in the new year."

Stan turned to leave, then paused, "What about the Christmas bonuses? You gave them before Christmas last year."

Barbara hated looking at the money-hungry ingrate before her. She was paying him more than enough money as it was. She smiled cynically. "Unless you can find us a way out of that healthcare disaster, I don't think I have money to pay bonuses."

Stan lowered his glance, turned, and quietly left.

* * * *

At 6:30 p.m., Barbara glanced up at the clock. She walked down the hall to Jerry Tracek's office. His light was out. *He better have done what I asked.* She went back to her office, told her secretary she could leave and left for her dinner meeting with Steve Garrity.

She rode the elevator alone, then walked through the lobby, waving to the security guard, then walked out the front door of the Eaton Center. The homeless woman, who hung out nearly every evening was there, leaning against the back wall of the cathedral near the dark driveway that ran between the cathedral and the Eaton Center. Though the woman's presence always subtly annoyed Barbara, once in a while she would give her some change, if she had any, as long as she also was not pressed for time.

The woman called out her usual crackling chant into the cold crisp air, "Can you help me?"

Barbara reached in her coat pocket. Nothing. She said, "I'm sorry, I don't have any change." Barbara turned away, then stopped. *It's cold, and it is almost Christmas.* She glanced at her watch. She had a minute to spare. She pulled up her purse and opened her pocketbook. She rummaged through the 20s and 10s and 5s until she finally reached some 1s. *"Thank God,"* she said to herself. She took out two dollars, closed her purse, and walked over. The woman looked like a real mess tonight. For the first time, too, Barbara realized she might be about the same age as her. Barbara handed her two dollar bills and said, "Merry Christmas."

Barbara didn't wait for a reply but turned and began walking away.

"Merry Christmas," the woman said, adding in an ominous tone, "Before it's too late."

Barbara stopped and quickly turned around, glaring, "What did you say?"

"I said Merry Christmas."

Barbara walked back up to her, with a scowl on her face, asking sternly, "You said something after that. What was it?"

The woman cowered, and said in her creaky voice, "I heard a woman say something, but it wasn't me."

"What did you hear? What woman?" Barbara demanded, cautiously glancing into the shadows.

"I heard a woman say, 'before it's too late.' It sounded like she was right behind me... I looked, but..." she turned, "No one was there."

"Where is she?" Barbara said, frightened now, looking around in the darkness of the late December evening.

The woman shrugged, "I told you. I didn't see her."

Barbara turned away and started walking as quickly as she could up Twelfth Street toward the Hoffbrau House Restaurant. Suddenly she stopped. She remembered: It was a dream, a week or so earlier. A woman's voice had spoken those words, no, chided her with those words. She had forgotten. Now, she shuddered and quickly turned around to make sure no one was following her. She picked up the pace and kept going. It felt more desolate tonight than any other time she could remember. No one was around as she headed along the sidewalk overshadowed by a long, darkened, downtown store that was already closed. The crisp cold air created a silence that yielded only to the pounding of her heels, as they echoed against the concrete buildings of the empty street. She suddenly wished she had not walked tonight.

A streetlamp ahead was out, and it unnerved her, she shuddered as she passed through the dark spot, and she forced herself to keep going. Something rattled not far behind her, and she turned abruptly, looking back. Nothing.

She then turned again and quickened her pace.

Finally, she reached the corner of the cross street, and turned onto it, sighing with relief. The cross street was well lit, and the Hoffbrau House Restaurant was now in sight.

When she finally arrived at the restaurant, she was short of breath and took a moment outside the door to collect herself. The voice, the dark walk, it had all really spooked her. She opened the door and stepped into the warmly lit, noisy entranceway, searching over the heads of the waiting patrons until she spotted Steve. She waved and Steve cut through the crowd to reach her. "Hello, Barbara. Glad you could make it. Our table is ready."

"Oh, wonderful. I am famished. It was a brisk walk over here."

"You walked?"

"Yes, I usually do. However, tonight I wish I had driven."

"Well, I'll drive you back after dinner."

"Thank you," she said, greatly relieved.

The dinner was tense. She could not relax completely. She was preoccupied, not only by what had been said near the Church but also by the foreboding sense of urgency she had felt all day.

After dinner, Steve dropped her at the entrance to the parking garage of Eaton Center. She walked up the cold concrete ramp and went to her car. It felt just as desolate as the walk to the restaurant, and she could not put her finger on why. She started her car quickly and immediately locked her doors. She drove out as fast as she could, weaving through the downtown streets just as quickly, until finally she reached the highway.

She exhaled loudly. As she drove past lamppost after lamppost along the highway; she began to think. Then, she began to worry. She knew the dream and the voice from the darkness were connected. So was the sense of urgency she felt all day.

They were all connected. *Too late for what?*

* * * *

When Barbara got home, her husband Todd was sitting in the living room reading. "Hi Todd," she said, as she stormed past him, "I have to do something." She went directly into her study and called her personal assistant.

"Martha. I need you to do some research about a dream for me. Look up what it means when someone hears the phrase in their dream, *"before it's too late."*

"Before it's too late, got it. Is that all?"

"Yes. Wait, no. What is happening tomorrow?"

"Umm, nothing new. We went over it all yesterday."

"I know that, Martha. I want to go over it again. What time is the chef coming?"

"He will be there at 3."

"What time are you bringing the gifts?"

"4:30."

"Okay, and what time is Santa coming?"

"At 7:30 for 30 minutes, and Christmas morning at 10:30 for 20 minutes."

"All right. Make sure you tell him to be ready to take pictures with all the grandchildren before he leaves. He missed one last year, and I heard about it all year long."

"I already told him."

"Did you wrap all the gifts yet?"

"I am still working on it."

"Well, are you going to finish on time?" Barbara was getting annoyed. This was supposed to be done yesterday.

"Yes, it will be finished. I am working on it right now as we speak."

"All right. Drop them off at 4:30 sharp and arrange them. Then get the chicken. Oh, and pick up some fries too."

"Fries too. Got it." Martha said.

"What about Christmas Day? Did you get the tickets for the Wonder Woman movie?"

"Yes, I have 22 tickets."

"Good, that should be enough. If I have extra, you can exchange them next week."

"Is there anything else?" Martha asked.

"No, that covers everything. Call me when you find out about the dream research."

"I will, but it may be tomorrow."

"Fine," Barbara said curtly. She hated the thought of having to wait. "I will talk with you tomorrow."

"Good night, Barbara."

Barbara closed the call and stared at the phone. Martha's subtle defiance had been coming through loud and clear lately. She would replace her on her own timetable, though, when it suited her.

* * * *

It was dark outside. Barbara turned on the light over her desk, grabbed her list of prospects, and took it with her into the living room, where Todd was still doing some work on his iPad. She slipped off her shoes and curled up on the couch next to him. She asked, "How was your day, honey?"

"Not too bad," he replied, lowering his glasses, "The judge ruled in my favor on the Murray case. So, I will be getting a nice payout on that in about two months."

"Really, how much?"

"My share will be close to $20,000."

"Oh, that's it? I thought you said this could be a big case."

Todd frowned some. "It's not chicken feed."

"Oh, I suppose," Barbara replied. Her opinion that his contribution to their finances was increasingly paltry compared to hers had resurfaced. In her mind, he needed to sharpen his game.

There was quiet for a few moments, then Todd asked, "Are you looking forward to seeing your Christmas gifts from the kids?"

"I strictly forbade anyone from buying me any gifts."

"Why?"

Barbara scoffed, "Because, Todd, I don't need Christmas gifts. I have Amazon and enough money to order whatever I want, whenever I want."

Todd nodded and shook his head, both at the same time. There was quiet for another few moments.

Todd looked up. "Oh. Your sister Gwen called."

"Oh, God," Barbara said, "Right before Christmas? They are probably just looking for a good meal."

Todd replied, "Well, she said they wanted to see us. She said the girls are all home."

"All? Including the junkie?"

"I guess. She said all, so I guess that includes Stephanie, though I don't know if she is still on drugs."

"What else would she be doing? None of them have a life." Barbara shook her head. "No. I am *not* inviting them here. It is too much work. Besides, when is the last time they had us over?"

Todd smirked, adding, "We wouldn't go anyway."

His response startled her.

It carried the weight of the urgency, which somehow connected to the foreboding feeling she had felt all day. It was as if their lives were racing to some dire place. Todd would never have spoken like that before. It was something she would have said. Hearing him say it surprised her.

Before it's too late.

Barbara's face donned a fake smile, and she said slowly, "I suppose we wouldn't."

Out of the corner of her eye, she watched Todd staring down at his iPad, immersed in his work. She felt lost for several moments, vulnerable, needing to feel loved, needing to feel like a woman, and not a business machine. She nestled up nearer to him. "Todd, do you want to go up to bed early?"

He glanced over at her, then down at her legs, then back up as if he were thinking. "Not tonight, Barbara. I have a lot of work to finish if I am going to get the money into our accounts before February."

She hid her disappointment. It was not the first time of late he had turned down her invite to head upstairs. Was he growing tired of her?

The phrase ran through her mind again. *Before it's too late.*

"I'm going to bed," she said. She grabbed her list and went upstairs to their room.

* * * *

Barbara sat on the edge of her bed, taking off the day's clothes, numbly putting on her pajamas. So much was bothering her. She turned on her light and perused her prospect list. She hated when Christmas fell in the middle of the week. It messed up two whole weeks of business. "Dammit," she said, slamming the papers on the bed. There was really no opportunity to reach her prospects or her new clients respectfully before Monday, January 6th. However, she would try to fit in a few key dinners.

She got up, took her sleeping pill, brushed her teeth, removed her makeup, then jumped into bed.

She waited for sleep, but it would not come easily. The feeling she had all day was gnawing at her. *Urgency for what? Before what's too late?* She rolled over on her side, thinking. She had felt a real fear tonight while talking with the homeless woman near the church. Fear had held no sway in her life in ages, and to suddenly experience it now alarmed her. The walk to the restaurant had downright frightened her too. She wanted to tell Todd, but he would not understand. She closed her eyes, trying to rationalize it away until finally, she drifted off to sleep.

During the night, an image flashed into her mind. It lasted only for a moment, but it came suddenly and was more real than she had ever dreamed before. She gasped out loud and sat up, heaving.

Todd turned on the lamp and sat up, "What happened?"

"I... I had a dream... Oh, my God... that scared me."

"What was it?" he asked in a half-asleep, half-alarmed tone.

Barbara swallowed, "It was my grandmother. She was standing right there, staring at me, with that wretched cross look of hers all over her face." Barbara pointed to the end of the bed. "Oh, God," she said, closing her eyes and letting her head fall back.

"Are you going to be okay?" Todd asked.

"Yes, I just need to relax for a little while. Go back to sleep."

Todd turned off the light and rolled over.

Barbara sat in the darkness, feeling more afraid than she ever had.

* * * *

The next morning was Christmas Eve. Barbara put on her new navy-blue pants suit and donned her red heels, then took down her matching purse from the closet. She wanted to look sharp today. Christmas Eve or not, she didn't want her workers thinking it was a day to slack off. Barbara had already made it clear to all that they were to treat it as a regular workday. There was far too much to do, especially before giving them the day off for Christmas.

She got in her car and drove downtown. As she was pulling around the corner toward the garage on Twelfth Street, she noticed what looked like a younger homeless man, harassing what looked like an equally young homeless woman. He was shouting at her, raising his arms. The woman was screaming, backing away, as if she feared the man. She also looked like she was pregnant. Barbara slowed and started to stop. She thought about calling 911, but someone behind her beeped, and she said, "Oh, screw it."

She pulled up the ramp into the parking garage. She pressed the button, took a ticket, and said to herself out loud, "They can solve their own problems. I don't have time for this today."

Strangely, her cousin Lori came to mind. She had heard Lori had become homeless or was about to. When they were young, they were friends, living not far from each other. Once Barbara's parents moved to the suburbs, they lost touch. Lori got involved in a gang, so Barbara heard. She had married, and divorced, and the last Barbara heard she was living with her 80-year-old mother. Lori had written to her a few months back, but Barbara chose to let that sleeping dog lie right where it was. She had no time for her.

Barbara put Lori out of her mind, and got out of her car, making her way into the building and into the elevator.

As the elevator doors were closing, a hand reached in to catch the doors at the last second, and they reopened. It was Jerry Tracek. "Oh, good morning, Barbara," he said with an obvious look of surprise on his face as he nervously got into the elevator. He stood in the front for a moment with his back to her, then backed up to one corner. She glanced over at him and asked, "Did you finish the proposal yesterday?"

Jerry swallowed, "I tried, Barbara. I was here until 6, but I had to go. My wife and I had to visit her mother, but I got here early to work on it."

Barbara did not reply. When they reached the 17th floor, the doors opened. Barbara walked out and said, "Bring it to my office."

"But I have to finish it," he said with a hint of desperation.

"You are finished with it. Bring it over now."

She walked away.

Minutes later as she sat in her office looking out over the roof of St. John's Cathedral, waiting. Her father came to mind again. How she missed him, but she would always be proud of him. He had turned his business into a profitable endeavor near the end of his life, ruling with an iron fist. She remembered when he told her, 'They must fear you, Barbara. Employees must know who the boss is. It is the only way to get things done right.' That was only weeks before he died suddenly, and she would never forget it.

There was a knock at her door. She turned around slowly, then stood up, ready to deal with her insubordinate associate.

Jerry walked in and stood in front of her desk with his knees slightly trembling. "Barbara, I was stuck on one part. I just needed to think it over. I can finish it now."

"No, Jerry. You are done working for me."

"But... but that's not fair. I have been doing a good job. Look at what I did on the Loktite proposal."

"Jerry, I don't count points by victories. I count by losses. You have too many losses in my books."

"Losses?"

"Losses, mistakes, missed deadlines, they all add up. Pack up your desk and leave."

"Barbara, please. What about all the things I have done well. I have done a good job with our clients. Please, Barbara, I need another chance."

"Sorry. Leave now, and I will not give you a negative reference."

"Wait a second," Jerry said, his tone suddenly turning adversarial, "When you hired me, we promised to give each other a month's notice. You can't just fire me without any notice? We agreed to give each other time. We said we would give each other a month."

"No. No. No. No. No, Jerry," Barbara said, wagging her finger like a pre-school teacher. "You are *done* working for me. Clean your desk out and get out! I will pay you through the end of the day."

Jerry shook his head, turned away slowly, and left.

Barbara buzzed her secretary. "Get Martha on the phone. And call Stan and remind him of the project I gave him."

"Right away, Barbara."

* * * *

Barbara turned toward the window wall with a sleek smile on her face. She said to herself, "Yes, it's a little too late for you, Jerry." She chuckled to herself as she looked out toward the western skyline, gazing out over the roof of St. John's Cathedral. She was glad to be rid of him.

The snow was falling, and it felt like Christmas for the first time since last year. She couldn't wait for the kids to see Santa Claus. She had paid a lot of money for this one, and he better do it right this year, or she was getting someone else.

The intercom startled her. "Martha is on the phone."

She turned and picked up the phone. "Martha, did you finish wrapping the gifts?"

"I am finishing as we speak."

Barbara pressed her lips together, then snapped, "You told me that last night."

"I am almost done. There are a lot of gifts."

"I know how many gifts there are, Martha. I had you buy them, didn't I?"

There was silence.

Barbara continued in a mocking tone, "I would know how many gifts there are. Right?"

"Right," Martha replied feebly.

"Enough about that. What did you find out about the dream?"

"It said a recurring dream, coupled with hearing a voice outside of the dream, could be construed as a warning from beyond."

"Warning. Are you sure?"

"That's what it said."

"Well, I need you to check on another dream. Pronto. I had a dream in which my grandmother was looking at me angrily. She was standing in my room. Just for a flash, though, and then she was gone."

"Did she say anything?"

"No, she didn't say anything. Don't you think if she said something, I would have told you?"

There was silence again.

Barbara snapped, "Just call me back."

Martha added, "I am going to finish the gifts first."

Barbara was silent for a moment, "Martha, I don't care what you finish first. Just get it all done." Barbara hung up.

* * * *

At 3:30 p.m., Barbara left the office. She walked out the front door of Eaton Center in hopes of finding the homeless woman. She had a dollar in her hand, but really, she wanted to find out if she had seen the man who had said those words. The woman was not there. Barbara walked around the building and went into the parking garage.

She drove home. On the way, her phone rang. She glanced at the screen mounted on the car holder. It was her sister Gwen. She hit the end button, sending her to voicemail.

A minute later, when the voicemail notification came up, she pressed play.

Barbara, Hi. This is Gwen. I wanted to wish you a Merry Christmas. Umm…Bob and I are having an open house the day after Christmas… in the evening, early. Uhhh, my girls are all at home, and we wanted to see you guys. I am making pizza like Mom used to make. Can you come? Call me.

Barbara hit delete. "Like Mom used to make. Right. In your dirty house! No thanks."

Barbara continued driving, thinking about her sister. She was angry that Gwen was so weak. She remembered the day her father had tried to teach them both a valuable lesson. Barbara was nine years old, and Gwen was a year younger. Barbara had gotten the lesson, but

Gwen... well, she was just Gwen. They were at Geauga Lake amusement park for her uncle's company picnic. At one point after the children's games, the company was handing out Fudgesicles to the hundreds of kids. Barbara had raced and pushed her way to the front to snatch one. Gwen, in her typical fashion, had been less assertive. When they got back to the picnic table area, Gwen was one of the only kids without a Fudgesicle. They had run out.

Barbara remembered how proud her father was of her, when he said in front of them both, "Barbara, let this be a lesson. You have to take what you want in life. Gwen, let this be a lesson to you too. No one is going to hand things to you in life. You have to go get them for yourself."

Oh, how Barbara wished Gwen had gotten the lesson. It would have made her life so much better.

* * * *

By the time she got home, it was nearly 4 p.m. She went upstairs, took off her pants suit, removed the rest of her clothing, and stepped into the shower. She turned on the hot water and put her head under the running water. *Oh, I need a break. I hate Christmas.* She lathered up and shampooed her hair, then rinsed off and stepped out and dried off. She put on sheer nylons, shimmied into her gold dress, and then put on her gold earrings and matching necklace. Lastly, she slipped into her black silk heels, applied her makeup, and inspected herself in the mirror. She was ready.

When she got downstairs, Todd was on the phone listening to someone. He held up his hand, signaling for her to wait a moment. Barbara half-smiled went to the kitchen, where the chef was busy getting the final dinner dishes ready. The large spacious kitchen looked like a restaurant and smelled marvelous. She could see the lobsters inside the pot of cold water. Next to them, on the stove, was a large pot with the fire going strong, readying the water, getting it to the needed boiling point.

"Everything looks fantastic," Barbara said enthusiastically.

"Barbara?" It was Todd calling from the living room. She went in, glancing at the corners of the house as she did, making sure the cleaning lady had done her job thoroughly enough.

"What is it?"

Todd was holding their home phone in his hand with his finger on the hang-up button. "That was a voicemail from your employee, Jerry."

Barbara's face narrowed, "What did he want?"

"He was begging for his job back. Did you fire him?"

"Yes, this morning."

"How come?"

Barbara sighed, "If you must know. He has been getting lax lately."

"But I thought he wrote the proposal for a big account you just got."

Barbara scoffed, "Oh, big deal. He also almost screwed another one up."

Todd said, "Barbara, it's Christmas Eve. Maybe you should give him a break. He left his number."

Her face narrowed again, "Look, Todd. Do I get involved in your business affairs?"

His eyes lowered, and he replied sheepishly, "No."

"Well then, don't get involved in mine."

Barbara turned and walked into the dining room, making sure the table had been set correctly. There were 16 place settings for the adults, and older grandchildren, along with a stack of plates for the younger grandchildren. They would fix their plates and sit around the living room.

She then went into the family room. The tree was set up perfectly in the center, and there were nearly a hundred gifts around it, jutting out in all directions. She carefully examined the gifts along the edges, scanning to make sure Martha had labeled them neatly. She wondered why Martha had not called about her dream. This bothered her, and she vowed to have a talk with her first thing the day after Christmas.

Barbara sat down, wishing she had a moment, any moment, to sit and not worry about anything.

* * * *

Soon after, the doorbell rang, and Barbara looked at the clock. It was 5:30. She leaned forward and saw the kids coming up the driveway. It was her oldest son, Matthew, and his wife Monica, and their three children.

She got up and went to answer the front door. She opened it, and said enthusiastically, "Come in, come in." She lowered her cheek for the grandchildren to kiss her, then hugged her daughter-in-law, Monica, and then her son. "You are just on time. Go into the family room. There are appetizers along the table."

"Thanks, mom," Matt said as he took off his coat. "Hey, do you think the kids can watch TV a little later? Monica's mom just dropped off *The Little Drummer Boy* on DVD. They have been begging me to watch it."

"No, I'm sorry Matt. Wait till you get home. We are on a very tight schedule. Besides, do you really want your children learning such fables?"

"Okay, no problem." Matt said.

Her youngest son and his family arrived next. Barbara greeted them with a smile, then glared at the half full driveway. Her youngest daughter, Dawn, and her family would not be coming until morning. Dawn's husband insisted they see his family every Christmas Eve.

Barbara groaned at the thought of keeping the show going for another long day.

She glanced at the clock. It was 5:50 p.m. *Where is Laura? If they are late because of church I am going to bust!* Moments later Laura and her family arrived. Barbara checked the time. It was 5:55 p.m. She smiled and waited by the door to greet them.

* * * *

With everyone present, the house was soon bustling. Barbara observed the chaos for a moment, then called everyone into the dining room. They sat down and waited while the chef brought out the main dishes, introduced each one, and offered Barbara to perform a taste test. As was her custom, Barbara tasted each dish, savored it for a moment, and then pronounced her approval. Only after the annual ritual of the tasting of the food was complete were all the dishes brought out and placed on the table.

Everyone enjoyed the meal, and all enjoyed the loud talking and laughing. After dinner, they retired to the family room to open gifts. Barbara led the way, intentionally clearing the dining room to allow her cleaning lady, Tia, to come in and begin clearing the table. Tia was middle-aged, a bit younger than Barbara. Barbara had found her at a party six years earlier and hired her on the spot. Tia was present, silently in the background, at most of Barbara's parties and family gatherings.

Within minutes, everyone anxiously gathered around in the large family room, waiting for Barbara to signal it was time. Suddenly, her cell phone rang. She had forgotten to turn it off.

Barbara looked down. It was Martha.

"Just a minute," Barbara said, walking out of the room.

"Martha, what are you calling for?" Barbara already knew why but she said it to make an excuse to the others.

"You wanted an answer on your dream. I looked it up. It said, she paused, 'It too is a warning from beyond.'"

Barbara felt her knees tremble, and she thought of Jerry, standing before her with his knees shaking, begging for mercy. Barbara anxiously asked, "What else did it say?"

"Well, it also said if a pattern of related dreams accompanies it, it could mean that disaster may be on the horizon."

The phrase ran through her mind again. *Before it's too late.*

"Dammit," Barbara said aloud. "I knew it. I am going to lose some of these new accounts."

"What?" asked Martha.

"Never mind. I will talk with you tomorrow night, Martha. We will have gift returns to make, I am sure of it, so plan on that the day after Christmas."

Barbara did not wait for her reply but hung up and went into the family room. "Okay, Laura, you can start handing out the gifts."

* * * *

After an hour of frantic gift opening, the melee was complete. Barbara glanced at her watch. It was time for Santa. Within a few minutes, the doorbell rang. Barbara jumped up, "Children, Santa is here!"

As most of the grandchildren jumped up too, the room exploded with excitement and followed Barbara to the door.

Santa came in, and he did a great job. He took pictures with all the kids and before long, the families began packing up their children and gifts. It took over a half hour to gather everyone up and get them out the door. Finally, everyone was gone, leaving Barbara and Todd alone.

Barbara sat in her living room, looking around at the cluttered house. She would have Tia come early and straighten everything out before her daughter Dawn arrived.

Todd sat down across from her. "Well, that went off perfectly."

"Yes, it did," Barbara said, scanning the room for her list of details she would give Tia. "I planned it very well this year." She paused, adding, "I am exhausted."

"Well, who wouldn't be."

Barbara's mouth tightened, "Now we have to go through it again for Dawn. I wish her husband would just cooperate."

"Well, let's try to understand," Todd said softly, "They have to visit his family too."

A feeling of utter emptiness formed in the pit of her stomach. "I hate Christmas," she lamented. "It's too much damn work. For what!"

Todd got up, saying, "I'm going to bed. Good night."

Barbara's eyes narrowed as she watched him walk away. She still wanted to talk, about the event, about the day, about anything. She suddenly felt very alone. Did Todd even care about her anymore? Was he going to leave her? She wouldn't put it past him. It didn't matter. He had not made her, and he could not break her. There were plenty of men who would kill to be with her.

The words came again. *Before it's too late.* She closed her eyes tightly and demanded loudly in her mind. *Stop!*

* * * *

The next morning Barbara woke early and inspected the dining room table where they would be having breakfast. Her housemaid and cook, Tia, was in the kitchen cooking the elaborate breakfast consisting of sausage, bacon, eggs, pancakes, toast, coffee, and juice.

"Good morning, Tia. How is everything going?"

"It is going very well, Barbara," she said cheerfully, "Merry Christmas."

"Oh, yes. Merry Christmas. Will everything be done on time?"

Tia nodded, smiling, "Yes, it will be ready."

"Good, thank you. After you clean up, you can go. Be here early tomorrow. I want that tree down."

"Are you sure?" Tia asked.

"Take it down tomorrow," Barbara said slowly. She lowered her eyes to meet Tia's, making sure they saw eye to eye on this important tenet of her plans.

Tia nodded again, half-smiling this time, and said, "I will."

Barbara raised her chin, and smiled confidently, and turned, leaving with the words, "Thank you."

* * * *

Within the hour, her daughter Dawn, her husband, and their four children, ages 7 to 12, arrived. After greeting each other, they sat down and enjoyed the breakfast Tia had prepared. Barbara watched with deep dissatisfaction. There was an emptiness to the whole affair she could not help but notice.

Tia brought out more toast and set down a small plate of the remaining eggs. Barbara tried to eat, but she felt too nervous. A throbbing headache was rearing up the back of her neck. She sipped her coffee, glancing at the clock, pleading for time to go faster. Then, her two youngest granddaughters began arguing about a toy. With each child's shriek, her headache intensified. She thought about the Advil in the upstairs bathroom and used it as an opportunity to excuse herself.

When she returned, they were still at it. "Girls, stop!" she snapped meanly.

Dawn looked up surprised, "Mom, are you okay?"

"Yes, just get them to quiet down."

Dawn grimaced and glared at her youngest. "Avery, stop it."

"But she won't give me my toy."

Barbara slammed her hand on the table. "Just stop!"

Everyone grew quiet. Barbara swallowed and tried to compose herself. She got up and took her coffee into the family room, saying, "Everyone finish eating and come into the family room."

Within a few minutes, Dawn and her family came back into the family room, where they began opening the remaining gifts. Barbara did not say much but just kept thinking about how she could not wait for it all to be over. The New Year held great hope for her business prospects. She was anxious to get back to it all. She would close out her profits for 2020 and set larger goals for 2021.

While they were waiting for Santa to arrive, Barbara sat next to Dawn on the couch in front of the Christmas tree. Avery came up to her. "Grandma, will you come to the Church with us on Tuesday?"

"Oh, I have a dinner meeting on Tuesday." Her eyes narrowed, "What time?"

"I don't know," Avery said, clasping her hands behind her back, swaying back and forth.

"It's at 7 p.m., mom. The First Communion Class and their families are going as a class for the Feast of the Holy Innocents."

"The what?"

"You know the Feast of the Holy Innocents. It is when Mary and Joseph escaped right before King Herod killed all the young children in Bethlehem."

Barbara watched her granddaughter's eyes sway over to her. She was clearly hoping that revelation might change her grandmother's mind. "Oh, I know what you are talking about. They just had something about that on the History Channel. Some scholars said they don't believe it ever happened."

"Mom!" Dawn protested, quickly taking Avery into her arms. "Grandma is busy, Avery. But don't worry, we will ask your other grandma to come."

"I don't see why going to Church in the middle of Christmas break is so important for a 7-year-old. What are these schools teaching kids anyway?"

"Mom!" Dawn said, glaring. She got up.

Barbara watched her turn away and wondered how her daughter could so easily buy into such fables, and worse, teach her children about them.

Suddenly, the doorbell rang. It was 10:30 a.m. Santa was back.

Barbara glanced at the clock and smiled. He was right on time. She stood up abruptly, "Children, guess who is here?"

The children ran to the door, knowing who it would be.

Before long it was over and Dawn's family left.

In the early afternoon, Barbara and Todd went to the movie theater to see Wonder Woman with most of their children. When she returned home in the early evening, it was already dark. She walked in, saying nothing, and went to bed, exhausted.

* * * *

The day after Christmas, Tia arrived early and began cleaning up. Barbara slept in until 8 a.m., then jumped up and showered. She dressed as sharp as ever, wearing a red pants suit, gold necklace, and dark black shoes. She needed to be at the office today. Everyone else would be there too, and she did not want to give any impression it was not a full workday.

She went downstairs and poured herself some coffee. Her phone rang.

"Hello Dawn," Barbara said, seeing the number on the phone.

"Hi Mom, I think Avery left her doll there."

Barbara shook her head, "Just a minute." She went into the back room and looked around. Avery's new doll was indeed lying on the floor behind the tree. "It's here."

"Okay, great. We will stop by later."

"I won't be home. I am heading to work. Hold on a second." Barbara called out to the kitchen, "Tia, I want that tree out on the front lawn and all these decorations put away this morning."

Tia nodded again, smiling, and said, "It is such a beautiful tree. Do you want to wait a few days?"

"Hold on," Barbara said. She turned Tia.

"Tia, as far as I am concerned, as soon as the six o'clock news came on TV last night, Christmas officially ended. That tree is lucky I even waited until this morning."

Barbara turned her attention back to the phone, "Okay, Dawn. I will leave the doll on the end table."

"Thanks, Mom. It sounds like you are busy over there."

Barbara was about to answer, but she stopped. She felt light-headed, and the room began to spin.

"Dawn… Dawn… I… I…"

"Mom!"

Barbara tried to open her mouth, but she fell straight forward onto her face.

"Mom!" Dawn's voice echoed faintly through the phone.

Barbara heard her, but then all went black.

Revelations

Barbara opened her eyes. She was inside a large, dimly lit room with a high ceiling. It was misty inside, but not wet, rather cloudy, hindering her ability to see. She looked down at her clothing. She was still wearing the red pants suit, gold necklace, and dark black shoes she had put on this morning. She heard a voice and wheeled around.

A taller woman was standing behind her with a grim look on her face. She had long, sand-colored, shoulder-length hair and was wearing, as near as Barbara could tell, some sort of costume. It was a white gown, a golden belt, and a golden laurel around her head. From her back, large, fake white wings protruded.

A tinge of fear shot through her mind. Barbara demanded: "Who are you, and where am I?"

The Angel did not smile, but replied, "You are at the place of first judgment where your destiny will be determined. I only hope it was not too late for you."

Before it's too late. Barbara's heart dropped into her stomach, and her chest tightened. She asked, through a suddenly labored breath, "Who are you?"

"I am Rosie, your Guardian Angel," she said, looking at her with kind yet distant eyes. "Your life as you knew it is over, Barbara."

"I want to go home," Barbara demanded.

"You have no home… yet. Where your home will be is being determined as we speak."

"You, listen to me," Barbara said, raising her finger, "I don't care what… "

"Silence!" Rosie said, interrupting her. We will wait for guidance from on high."

Suddenly, Barbara could not speak. Rosie pointed to two wooden chairs and motioned for Barbara to sit. She sat next to her, and they waited.

* * * *

Rosie sighed. She looked up, wondering what was taking so long. Rosie was a Host Commander in the Third Heavenly Realm led by Michael the Archangel. She rarely took assignments as a Guardian Angel, but this was an exceptional case. Barbara's old Guardian Angel had reported directly to Rosie. One day he threw up his hands, saying he feared without a change, Barbara would end up being condemned, and he asked Rosie to step in. She reluctantly agreed.

In the beginning, she liked Barbara, though she had to admit Barbara was horrid in almost every way. But she saw something in Barbara, and she resolved to turn things around quickly.

That was three years ago, and things had only gotten worse.

Rosie had not expected Barbara to have the stroke. Angels did not know the future of anything, much less what might happen to one of their charges, or for that matter, when they would die. It was part of the mystery of life, part of the mystery of good and evil.

She had hoped Barbara would be spared from going to a place of everlasting despair. Still, now, with Barbara suddenly being here in the place of judgment, she was afraid of what her judgment would be.

They waited.

* * * *

Finally, she heard the summons and looked up as if receiving a message. Her face lit up, but only for a moment. She turned to Barbara, lowered her chin, and peered into Barbara's eyes, saying, "It has been decreed that you will be shown the lessons of the Twelve Days of Christmas, all of which show one how to live. Afterward, and not until then, your fate will be determined."

Barbara protested loudly, "What? What lessons do I need? This is ridiculous!"

"Barbara, your life on Earth has been a mockery of what is important. It has been decreed that you are to be shown why before receiving your judgment."

She tried to speak again, but she could not.

"Behold," Rosie said as she waved her hand.

* * * *

Barbara and Rosie were suddenly standing alone in her family room, in front of her Christmas tree. Barbara thought, *Why hasn't Tia taken down the tree?*

Barbara stepped forward and examined it closely. It had never seemed so beautiful. Standing in the empty room, with the countless gifts from the day before now gone, was refreshing. She turned to look behind her. The dining room table was cleared. She looked into the front room. Nothing. There was no trace of Christmas anywhere in the house, except for the decorated Christmas tree, standing like a lone sentinel.

Barbara drew her attention to beneath the tree. She had not noticed at first, but there were a number of small square boxes under the tree. Each of them was the size of a grapefruit. All were precisely the same size, neatly wrapped, but with different colored wrapping paper and different colored bows. Barbara quickly scanned the neatly arranged long row and counted them.

There were 12.

She tried to speak but could not.

Rosie pointed at the 12 gifts. "These are lessons of the Twelve Days of Christmas that I, as your Guardian Angel, have chosen just for you. They are lessons that are meant to help you to understand. They are lessons for good, Barbara, as well as lessons of caution, but they all have two central themes."

Rosie paused.

Barbara folded her arms across her chest, "What themes?"

"The first, is that they are lessons in keeping Christmas well and the second is…" Rosie said, raising her finger slightly, "And the second is…"

"And the second is what?" Barbara asked, puzzled as to why she stopped.

Rosie raised her eyes, and seemed to be searching for the answer, until her eyes widened, signaling she had found it. "Oh, yes. Sorry…it slipped my mind. And…the second is… that they are lessons in keeping life well. Sorry about that." Rosie straightened up, "Now, are you ready for your first lesson?"

Barbara grew fearful, but she nodded. She had not been told what to do in a long time. Now, she was being forced to do something against her will. The feeling of powerlessness, of not being able to direct her own course was suddenly scaring her.

"Wait!" Barbara demanded. "What does Christmas matter! It's only one damn day!"

"Christmas cannot be contained in a day, Barbara. For thousands of years, it has been celebrated over 12 days. Sadly, this tradition has been forgotten in the modern age. Even so, as you will see, there is much more to Christmas than even that."

Barbara's face showed she didn't buy it.

Rosie ominously lifted her arm and pointed, "Take the first gift and open it."

Barbara reluctantly stepped forward and picked up the first gift. She slowly unwrapped it, periodically glancing up at Rosie. She wondered if she was dreaming and desperately tried to close her eyes and wake, but she could not. She continued until the wrapping fell away, and she cautiously opened the lid of the tiny white box.

Suddenly the room began to spin. She grabbed onto the Angel's arm as a bright light flashed. In the next instant, a date and place flashed into Barbara's mind, and then it was silent.

December 25th 1918
Detroit Mercy Hospital Pandemic Ward
The First Day of Christmas

Barbara found herself standing next to the Angel Rosie in a large, old-style hospital ward with a wooden floor and high white ceilings. She looked around, then looked at Rosie, hoping she would explain what was happening. But Rosie only said, "Barbara, this is the first story that has a lesson for you."

The date at time were firmly etched in her mind. Barbara scoffed, "What can the year 1918 possibly teach me?"

"Christmas is not bound by time nor place. Be silent and observe everything. Let nothing escape your notice."

* * * *

Caroline, a young woman in her mid-20s, stood next to the single framed metal bed, looking down at her fiancée, John. She had fallen in love with him on the first day they laid eyes upon each other, only seven months earlier. At that time, the world and the future lay wide open before them, and they had made plans to marry within the year. But that was before the Spanish Flu had begun to ravage the world. Now, their lives and everything they had dearly hoped for was suddenly changed.

Caroline bent down closer and whispered, "You made it to Christmas, John. Perhaps you will get through this after all," she said, with her voice full of hope.

"I don't know, Caroline," he replied. "I want to believe that."

"The doctor said if you made it to Christmas, you'd have a good chance of going home. Perhaps," she said smiling. "Perhaps we will be married in the Spring just like we planned. Oh, John, please try."

John had contracted the flu only 10 days earlier. He had been in this hospital ward for seven days now. He reached up and took her hand, "Darling, I want that… I do…" He started coughing, covering his mouth. He closed his eyes, trying to recover from the episode. He looked to his left, at the other beds in the ward. Some of them lay empty, with their linens removed and the pillowcases removed, taken away to be burned. One of the empty beds had held someone he had gotten to know. His name was Geoff, and he had gotten the flu only five days earlier. He had been carried in by his brothers, who left him with the nurses in the ward. They had not been back since. John had spoken to him a few times, but within three days, Geoff was unable to talk due to his labored breathing.

John had heard Geoff's final gasps the night before, and he listened to the nurse trying to comfort him. She was sweet, and kind, and loving in her words for a man she knew not. When he finally died, John heard her cry.

He looked back up at Caroline, knowing her heart needed to hear reassurance. "I will try to hold on. I will, for us." He started coughing again, with his chest heaving dramatically. He looked out the window across the ward. A gentle snow was falling, fluttering down against the gray sky's backdrop and brick hospital building across the courtyard.

"You better," she said, grasping his hand tightly and catching a tear that was rolling down her cheek.

John smiled, coughing slightly, trying to hold it back. "I so wanted to see you at Christmas. You look so pretty in your red bonnet."

"Oh, John, I love you."

"Caroline, no matter what, I will cherish this Christmas, because… because I love you, and…. this is our first Christmas."

"Oh, John," Caroline said, as she leaned forward and pulled her mask below her nose, then further to below her lips. She warmly kissed him on the side of his head, knowing it was all she could do. She whispered, "Merry Christmas, my dear John."

Just then, another woman walked into the ward. She was wearing a brown button-up overcoat and a brown hat that tied around her chin. She smiled at Caroline and John, wiped her feet, and removed her hat. She reached into her pocket and placed a mask over her face. From her other pocket, she took out a handful of small cloth crosses. She went to the first bed on the other side of the ward and spoke a few words to the man. She handed him a cross, and they held hands, praying for a moment.

The woman then went to the next bed, nodding, greeting the man with a smile. The man coughed several times, unable to return the greeting until finally, he stopped. He looked up at her, and a smile came over his face. They, too, exchanged some words, and she also handed him a cross. They then joined their hands and said a prayer together. The woman smiled at the man, said something, then moved down the ward past two empty beds. She paused in front of one, lowered her head, and whispered a prayer, then continued her way down the long line of beds to the next man.

"Who is she?" Caroline asked.

"No one special. She lives across the street and comes here every few days."

Caroline marveled at her, "That is very kind of her to take the time to come here."

John nodded, a tear coming from his eye, as he not only feared his future, he feared how Caroline would cope with what might happen in the next few days. But he could not show her his fear now. He smiled at Caroline and said, "Yes, it is very nice of her to visit us. She is an Angel."

John squeezed Caroline's hand and said, "Go home now, honey. I am going to rest."

"All right. I will see you tomorrow."

John smiled and watched her walk away. He realized he might never see her again. He called out, "Caroline?"

She turned.

"I love you," he said, feebly waving.

She blew him a kiss and turned and left.

* * * *

The scene started to fade from Barbara's vision. Rosie turned to her, asking, "What did you learn, Barbara?"

Barbara lowered her eyes, and her face grew perplexed, "I don't know. I saw that he was very sick. It was nice his girlfriend was there. What was I supposed to learn?"

Rosie quietly said, "Did you notice the courage of both of these women who were visiting the sick, even though they were in the middle of a pandemic. It greatly encouraged these men, and for some of them it would be the last human kindness they would know."

"Yeah, so? What does this have to with me?"

"Do you know anyone in the hospital who could have used some cheering up? Maybe even someone who made poor choices?"

Barbara realized Rosie was speaking about her nephew who was in the hospital. Barbara shook her head and protested, "Listen. It's not my fault that he…"

Rosie waved her hand, and, again, Barbara was unable to speak. She lifted her arm into the air, and they faded back to Barbara's family room. They were again standing in front of the Christmas tree, looking at the 11 remaining gifts.

Barbara slowly glanced up at her with her lips pressed tightly together.

Rosie asked, "Are you ready for the lesson of the Second Day of Christmas?"

Barbara again tried to speak, but she could only nod. She looked around and looked back toward the dining room. She wanted to stay here in her home. She wanted to run upstairs into her husband Todd's arms and beg him to protect her from the terrible Angel, but somehow, she could not. Somehow, she was… not there. She shook her head, trying to figure it out, trying to understand how this could be happening.

Rosie pointed toward the gifts.

Barbara reluctantly stooped down and reached under her tree and picked up the Second Gift. As she unwrapped it, she felt the tears running down her face. She wanted it all to end. Suddenly, the room began to spin. She reached for the Angel's arm, and the flash of light came as a date and place flashed into her mind.

December 26th 2020
Garfield Heights, Ohio
The Second Day of Christmas

Barbara found herself standing next to Rosie in the corner of her sister's kitchen. "Why are we here? Of all places?" Barbara looked around disgusted. "I hate coming here. This kitchen is so old and unkept!"

"It is not unkept at all, Barbara. It is lived in by a loving family. Now, watch."

* * * *

Barbara's sister Gwen hung up the phone near the kitchen table. "Well, I left another message."

Stephanie scoffed, "They are not coming. They think they are better than us."

"Stephanie, now stop that. It's not true."

"It is to, true. I see it all over Aunt Barbara's face every time we see her."

Gwen smiled and walked over to her husband George, taking him by the arm. "We have each other, and that is all we need. Now, let's eat!"

Gwen's daughters, Stephanie, Michelle, and Eve were all at the kitchen table waiting for their dad to cut up Gwen's homemade pizza.

"Hand me that pizza cutter, Gwen."

"Here ya go!"

George flipped it into the air, "And now, for my next trick, I will cut this pizza up!'

"Finally," Stephanie said.

As George began rolling the cutter through the thick dough, there was a knock at the kitchen door. Everyone turned. Gwen opened the door, "Mr. Cassidy! How are you?"

"Oh, not bad. I was out walking and saw the lights on."

"Come in, come in. We are just about to have some pizza."

"Hello, everyone," Mr. Cassidy said heartily.

George replied, "Sit down, John. Sit down right there next to Michelle."

"Okay, if you are sure, you have enough."

"We have plenty," said Gwen.

The pizza was cut, and slices were handed all around. The eating, and smiling, and laughing began.

Then, the phone rang. "Hello," Gwen said as she picked up the receiver. "Oh, hi, Norb. What are you and Vi doing?" A pause.

"Oh, okay. Why don't you stop over? We are about to sing some Christmas Carols. Yes, and I have some of mom's famous pizza. There is plenty….. Okay, see you soon."

She hung up, exhaling loudly. "Well, the party is growing by the minute. George. Let's roll out another pizza and get it in the oven. The Longs are on their way over."

Stephanie asked, "Mom, can I invite Jessica Cooper over?"

"Sure, the more, the merrier."

Within a half-hour, everyone gathered into the small living room where a warm crackling fire was waiting. They crowded onto the couches, armrests, and chairs around the Christmas tree.

Gwen handed out the song sheets to everyone.

"All right, is everyone ready?"

Gwen looked around at the smiling faces. "Okay, from the top."

She held up her song sheet and started them out, singing the opening line of the first song, 'Hark the Herald Angels Sing.'

One by one, her children and friends joined in. Soon, the small room was alive with the song. Gwen immediately began the next song, singing the words, 'Joy to the World, the Lord is come.'

Right away, everyone joined in. Laughter and smiles filled the tiny living room. Gwen stood up and announced, "All right, everyone, we have one more song, but it's not on the sheet. Don't worry though, I think you all know it."

Gwen started slowly, "You know Dasher... and Dancer... and Prancer... and Vixen... Comet and Cupid and Donner and Blitzen... but do you recall... the most famous reindeer of all?"

Stephanie added, "Badop bop bop," And all began, "Rudolph, the Red-Nosed Reindeer..." At once, everyone joined in the song, tapping their feet, and swaying back and forth.

Afterward, the friends left, and the girls went to bed, leaving Gwen and George sitting alone on the couch. Gwen held George's arm tightly and said, "George, that was wonderful."

"I know. It was special. I am so glad Stephanie is here with us."

Gwen looked up at him, her face sad, "I am too, George. We can only hope and pray she gets through this."

George patted her shoulder, "She will, Gwen. She will."

Gwen looked up into his eyes and raised her eyebrows, saying, "Well, I think we should retire early?"

George kissed her, then smiled, "My thoughts exactly."

* * * *

Barbara and Rosie stood in the living room of Gwen's house, next to her tree. Barbara noticed it was not nearly as elaborate as hers, and yet, in its simplicity, it seemed far more beautiful. She watched Gwen and her husband lovingly go up the stairs hand in hand. It reminded her of how far she and Todd had drifted. Barbara glanced over at Rosie. Her face seemed to show she understood Barbara's feelings.

Rosie asked, "Do you remember the old days, singing as a family?"

Barbara turned to her, half frowning. She lowered her glance, nodding. She remembered her grandparents, parents, and brothers and sisters singing Christmas carols together so long ago. She had forgotten how special it was to do so. She had not brought this tradition into her married life.

It had been left behind like so much else.

Rosie said, "Gwen has tried to honor your parents' ways."

This struck a wrong chord in Barbara. Anger instantly welled up, and she snapped, "Well, where did it get her? Look at this tiny old house. None of her children are successful. Stephanie is nothing more than a junkie."

"What is successful, Barbara? They are not rich, but there is a lot of love here. And Stephanie is trying very hard to overcome her addiction."

"Trying? Did I tell her to *try* drugs? Oh, and you're wrong about my father. He wised up, in case you didn't know, Rosie. He finally put his business profit first and his family's needs before the workers. It was only then we left poverty behind."

"Wised up? Is that when you decided to leave the good things behind too?"

Barbara started to reply, but she didn't know the answer.

Before they left, her sister's phone rang. Barbara saw the hall light turn on, and Gwen came out of her room and ran downstairs to answer the phone. "Hello?"

"Dawn, what is it? Why are you calling so late?" Gwen said nervously.

There was a long pause.

"What! I will be right over."

Gwen ran upstairs. "Everyone, wake up. Something has happened to Aunt Barbara."

George ran out of the room, "What happened?"

Stephanie and the girls came out of their rooms, too. "Mom, what happened?"

"Dawn didn't want to tell me on the phone, but she told me to come right over. Let's pray right now."

Barbara watched from the bottom of the stairs, as Gwen and her family gathered in a small circle at the top of the stairs. They all closed their eyes and said together the Our Father and a Hail Mary.

Barbara looked at Rosie, as her face turned ashen white, and a pit formed in her stomach. The realization that something had happened to her hit her again. This was no dream. It was real. She had died.

Rosie lowered her glance and looked into the sky. She raised her arm, and they were back in Barbara's family room, standing before her Christmas tree and the 10 remaining gifts. Rosie pointed.

Barbara wiped a tear, shaking inside, and said, "I am done with this charade."

"No, we are not done. Trust me. We must go on."

Barbara looked at her wondering if it was time to put her foot down and put a stop to it. She decided it was not time... yet. She sighed, and slowly picked up the next gift, unwrapped it, and opened the box. The room began to spin, and she grabbed Rosie's arm.

The date and place flashed.

December 27th 1984
Cincinnati, Ohio
The Third Day of Christmas

Suddenly, Barbara and Rosie were standing in the corner of the nearly empty dining room of what looked like a poorly kept inner-city nursing home.

"What are we doing in this dismal place? It smells," Barbara said, wincing.

"There are lessons for you here, Barbara. In some of these lessons, time and days will pass quickly, almost as if you are watching scenes change in a movie. Watch carefully as each lesson unfolds. In all the lessons, what you need to know will be revealed."

Barbara exhaled loudly, looking around the badly outdated dining hall with a few old people scattered around, most with their heads down, most staring into oblivion. One woman caught her eye. She looked too young to be there. She was talking with another woman who was wearing a business suit.

* * * *

Patty Brown sat up as straight as she could in her wheelchair. Her oxygen tube was fitted to her nose and hanging properly on her ears. She wanted to remove it but couldn't. This conversation was too important. She needed to show she would follow whatever rules were needed to be followed.

Before her sat a woman named Jan from the State of Ohio Department of Aging. Jan was a Patient Advocate. She looked much younger than Patty and had tan skin, long black hair, and brown framed glasses. She had her pen in one hand as she perused the standard forms on the table in front of her, carefully checking the boxes to document all of Patty's complaint.

But this was more than a complaint in Patty's mind. It was a deep need, which had to be fixed because Patty knew only one thing. She needed to get out of there.

Patty was 54 years old. She was on the thinner side, with fair skin and short reddish-brown hair. Over the last few years, her facial muscles had taken on a perpetual worried look.

She was still pretty, some would say, at least on days when she had the strength to fix herself up. She needed a wheelchair to get around now, with a small oxygen tank in tow.

Jan, the woman from the state, glanced at one of the forms, flipped it over, and without looking up asked, "So, why do you feel that you are being held against your will?"

Patty fumbled with her thoughts, knowing how important her answers were. She wished the woman was looking at her. This was too important to say to someone who didn't seem engaged. Patty felt stuck, but her pause caused the woman to look up. Patty had rehearsed this in her mind all week, now the pressure of the moment was causing her to falter. She forced herself to start, "Because!" she said, pausing again, her words feeling trapped. Finally, she blurted out, "They're not listening to me. I don't need to be here. I… I only came here because I was in the hospital. It was only supposed to be for a few weeks."

Jan nodded indifferently, looked down at the report, and said, "I see you arrived here 10 months ago."

"That's what I mean," Patty said finally hearing words that might lead to the empathy she desperately needed right now.

Jan continued to read, "It says here, there is no family at home. Did you live alone?"

"My mom died last year. I was living with her. But my husband… he… he is coming home in January."

Jan's brow furrowed, "Where is your husband?"

Patty's face scrunched up tightly. She hated when she had to answer questions about him, especially now. She took a deep, labored breath, and said, "My husband has been in jail for three years, but he is getting out in January."

Jan's face showed even more concern.

Patty hastily added, "I've been talking to him. We're going to… you know… be living together. I need to be there at home with him."

Patty had tried to make her case with Patient Advocates before. She was sure she could live on her own, but they would not approve her for that. Her husband's pending release was her last chance.

Jan nodded, sitting back, and exhaling slowly through pursed lips. "I see," she said. She checked off a few more boxes on her form.

"No, he really is coming home," Patty insisted.

"I believe you," Jan said, half smiling, her eyes doing a final check up and down the form. She looked up, "We will have to get more information."

Patty knew this was the moment of truth. She leaned forward, her eyes wide, her desperation no longer concealed. "You can call the prison. I have the phone number and his inmate number. They can give him a message to call you… since this is so important."

"All right," said the young woman. "Give me the information, and I will contact him."

Patty's eyes widened, "Wait here." She grabbed the wheels of her wheelchair and thrust herself back away from the table, using her feeble arms as best she could to wheel herself out of the dining room and down the long hallway to her room. She stopped halfway and closed her eyes. Her heart was racing too fast, and so was her breathing. She shuddered, trying to draw in oxygen, starting to feel a sense of panic, not only for her breathing but for her chances to convince this woman to help her.

"Patty, are you okay?" It was Deena, her friend from across the hall.

Patty looked up with labored eyes, unable to speak. She lifted her hand, pointing to her room.

"You want to go to your room?"

Patty nodded.

Deena wheeled her the rest of the way and waited until Patty retrieved her husband's information, neatly folded into a small square piece of paper. Deena wheeled Patty back to the dining room where Jan was waiting.

Patty said, "Here. Just call the Warden's office and leave a message."

The woman took the paper, copied down the information, and then put her forms and pen away. She smiled professionally and said, "I will process all of this, and we will get back to you."

"When?"

"Oh, I believe in a few weeks at the most."

"Can't… can't you do anything sooner?" Patty pleaded now. It was the only thing left that she could do.

The woman smiled with tightened lips, "We will do our best, but these things take time."

Patty looked away, wanting to scream, wanting to demand they release her now. She couldn't though. As Jan walked away, tears began falling down Patty's cheeks, finding their way down the same path her private tears had traveled for months now.

* * * *

Later that night the aide came in and helped Patty get undressed and into bed. Patty laid awake, staring at the white ceiling, thinking back. She never used to need help, not before she went into the hospital almost a year earlier. She had come down with pneumonia and at the end of her hospital stay, a social worker determined she was too weak to go home right away and needed rehab in a nursing home. When she arrived at the nursing home, she was able to dress herself, but needed the use of a wheelchair only when she was tired. The therapy was supposed to get her stronger, to get her ready to go home, but things had gone downhill since then.

There was a knock at the door. "Who is it?" Patty asked from her bed.

"It's Deena. Can I come in?"

"Sure," Patty said.

Deena had been her friend for almost two months now. She was the same age as Patty. There was nothing wrong with her physically. She had been ordered to come here for substance abuse rehab. Patty liked her a lot because she and Deena were not like many of the other residents, who were very old. Most of them were never getting out, but she and Deena were getting out. They were going home, and they had become kindred spirits in this hope.

Deena pulled up a chair, "So how did it go with the advocate?"

"I don't know," Patty said, wishing to change the subject. Patty pivoted, "How about you? Any news about getting out of here?"

Deena's normally cheery countenance changed as she shook her head, "They told me I have to stay an extra two months. Those idiots said I am not participating in the therapy. It's such B.S."

"That sucks," Patty said.

Deena shrugged, "I guess it's okay. I have nowhere to go now anyway."

Patty yawned, "I'm sorry, Deena."

Deena smiled the brave smile Patty always loved to see and said, "You get to sleep. I'll see you tomorrow." Deena got up and left, returning to her room across the hall.

* * * *

The next day, after having breakfast in the dining room, one of the nurse's aides came in. "Patty, you have a phone call."

Patty's heart began to race. It had to be her husband. She pulled her wheelchair back from the table and began heading to the phone situated in the middle of the dining room. Very few of the residents had phones in their rooms, and it was here Patty had to take phone calls.

The aide waited until she got over to the phone. "Okay, Patty, I am going to go and transfer it."

"Okay," Patty said, nervously fidgeting with her oxygen tube, wondering what she was going to say, wondering what she had to say.

The phone rang. Patty quickly picked up. "Hello?"

"Patty, this is Jimmy." His voice sounded worn. "I was calling to say Merry Christmas."

"Christmas was two days ago, Jimmy. I thought you weren't going to call."

"I couldn't get a chance on the phone. I just got one today." His voice now sounded annoyed. It worried her.

"Oh well, Merry Christmas, Jimmy. I miss you."

There was a pause. He then asked, "How are you doing?"

"I'm doing fine. I am getting better. I want to start our life again. When are you getting out?"

"Oh, sometime in February."

"February! I thought it was January?" Her voice trailed off in deep disappointment.

There was another pause. Then he said, "It got moved."

"To when? Do you know the date?" Patty knew that he knew the exact date.

"Uhhh, I think around the 15th, give or take."

TWELVE DAYS • 54

"Well, our house is still there. I am pretty sure of it."

There was another uncomfortable pause, longer this time. "Patty, I am not so sure I am coming home. A lot has changed. I've changed. You've changed too. Look, you are in a nursing home and in a wheelchair."

"I'm getting stronger, Jimmy. I am going to be fine. We are going to be fine. We can help each other like we used to."

"Yeah, I will think about it."

"Jimmy, please. Look, some woman named Jan from the state is going to be calling. Just tell her that we are going to live together."

"Uhhh, I will think about it. I told you. Now stop insisting." The tone of his voice betrayed his true feelings.

"Jimmy, listen."

"I gotta go, Patty. I will call you."

"Jimmy, no. Listen, don't hang…"

He hung up.

Patty's mouth dropped open, and her eyes fell downward to the floor. It suddenly hit her that she was never getting out of there.

She was only 54 years old, and she was never getting out. She lifted her head and glanced around the dining room at the residents who were still at the table, the ones who were not strong enough to leave on their own. Many were sleeping. Some only stared blankly ahead. A few were looking at her and had probably been listening to her call. She set the phone down and numbly wheeled herself down the long hallway to her room. She maneuvered herself next to the bed, stood and then laid down. She pulled the covers over her head and began to cry harder than she ever had.

* * * *

That afternoon there was a knock at her door. "Patty? Can I come in?"

She recognized the voice. It was the tall man who visited the residents every week. He carried a few bags with him. It seemed each time he visited he brought more and more. The bags were filled with cans of soda and chips and Twinkies. Patty labored to sit up. "Come in," she said.

The man came in, as Patty turned, to sit on the edge of her bed. "Merry Christmas, Patty. How are you doing?"

"Not too good," she said, her breath very labored today.

"Oh, what's wrong?"

"My husband… he's acting like an idiot," she said, laboring to get the words out. Patty had been telling this man of her plans to go home for the last few months. He and Deena were the only ones who believed her.

"I brought you some snacks," the man said as he pulled up a chair. He pulled out two cans of pop, and two Twinkies, and two small bags of chips.

"Thank you," she said. "Put them in that drawer, please." She pointed to the drawer next to her bed. She was too tired to do it herself.

The man did, but instead of getting up to leave, he paused, and looked at her, and asked, "You seem really sad."

His words disarmed her, and her tears began to well up again. "I need to get out of here."

The man nodded, thinking, then asked, "Can we say a prayer together?"

They had said a prayer together once or twice before, but never while she was in this state. Patty wiped her eyes, "Yes, I would like that."

They joined hands and closed their eyes. The man said, "Heavenly Father, we pray that you will help Patty. You can see how desperate she feels. You know her heart and her heart's desires. I pray that in this season of Christmas, you will help her and give her what she needs the most." He then started the Our Father. Patty joined him,

TWELVE DAYS • 56

"Our Father, who art in Heaven, hallowed be thy name. Thy kingdom, come. Thy will be done. On Earth, as it is in Heaven. Give us this day, our daily bread, and forgive us our trespasses, as we forgive those who trespass against us. And lead us not into temptation but deliver us from evil."

Patty paused, keeping hold of his hand, hoping for this prayer to be answered.

The man let go and said, "All right, Patty. I will be back on Sunday."

"Are you a minister?" she asked.

He smiled, shaking his head, "No, I am just a plain old Catholic, just like you, Patty."

"Thank you," she said.

The man stood up, nodded reassuringly to her one more time, and left.

* * * *

The following evening, Deena was sitting up in her bed watching a Year in Review special on TV. Suddenly she saw the nurse racing past her door with a breathing machine. Deena went out into the hall to see what was happening. They were going into Patty's room. Deena went over.

"What's going on?" she asked.

The nurse, a tall black woman who worked through an agency a few nights a week, turned, "Patty is having trouble breathing."

Deena looked in and saw Patty laboring to breathe. Her face was anxious, frightened as she watched the nurse and aide fix the oxygen mask onto her and turn on the machine, adjusting the oxygen level.

The nurse said firmly, "Keep breathing, Patty…. That's it."

Finally, Patty seemed to start to get some breaths. It took a while longer, but the panic subsided, and Patty began to breathe. The nurse covered her up with the blanket and tucked her in. She said, "Patty, we are going to call Dr. Fawzy to let me know what is going on."

Patty nodded with her eyelids, and she drifted off to sleep.

When the nurse left, Deena went in to sit by her. She sat for a while, softly humming a few Christmas songs. At one point, Patty opened her eyes and offered the hint of a smile.

"Hi, Patty. How are you feeling?"

Patty shook her head slowly. She said, from under the mask, "I like that song."

"Which one?"

"Noel," Patty said, barely perceptible.

Deena smiled widely and replied, "It is one of my favorites too."

Deena paused, thinking, then began to sing softly,

"The first Noel, the angels did say
Was to certain poor shepherds, in fields as they lay:
In fields where they lay keeping their sheep
On a cold winter's night that was so deep
Noel, Noel, Noel, Noel
Born is the King of Israel!

They looked up and saw a star
Shining in the east, beyond them far
And to the earth, it gave great light
And so, it continued both day and night
Noel, Noel, Noel, Noel
Born is the King of Israel!"

Deena stopped, smiling, "That's all I know, Patty."

Patty reached up and brushed the tears falling down her face. "I loved that." She closed her eyes tightly and said, "I can't stay… here… I want… to… go…home."

"Oh, Patty, you will go home…"

Patty shook her head, then, her eyes suddenly widened, as she gasped, "I… can't… breathe."

Deena ran down the hall. "Nurse! Nurse! Patty needs you!"

The nurse quickly ran down the hall into the room. Patty was laboring hard. The nurse shouted, "Patty, it is okay. Patty, just breathe. Just breathe."

Deena came up next to her, "Take a breath, Patty. It's okay." Deena could see Patty was panicking. The nurse grabbed her phone from her pocket and dialed 911. "This is Nurse Robbins from West Side. I need an ambulance stat. The patient is unable to breathe."

Deena shouted in desperation, "Patty, just breathe!"

Patty grabbed Deena's hand tightly, her eyes pleading, and squeezed as hard as she could.

* * * *

The following morning, the tall man came in with his bags of pop, Twinkies, and chips. He went around the lobby, hall, and dining room, handing out requested items to the residents he had gotten to know over the last year. Finally, he got to Patty's room. He peaked in. The bed was empty, and there were no sheets or blankets on it. He stepped out and checked the room number, thinking he had the wrong room. Then he heard someone behind him. He turned.

It was Deena.

"Oh, hi Deena. Where is Patty?"

"Didn't you hear the news?" Deena said, looking helplessly into the empty room.

"No, what news?"

Deena stepped closer, and took hold of his hand, and said softly, "Patty died."

"Patty died? What!… when?" His voice trembled.

"Last night," Deena said, wiping a tear from her eye.

The man sighed heavily, shaking his head. He went into Patty's room and sat on her empty bed. He began to weep. Patty had wanted to get out of there desperately, and she never made it.

He stayed for a few minutes, letting his emotions flow, saying a prayer for her soul. Then, he slowly got up and left.

* * * *

In the corner of the room, Patty sat in her wheelchair next to her Angel, watching the tall man. She looked up at the Angel and said, "He and Deena were the only ones who cried for me."

"Yes," the Angel said, "They both cared about you, Patty." He paused, "Are you ready?"

"Where are we going?"

The Angel reached out his hand and helped her to stand up from her wheelchair. Then, he waved his hand in a wide circle. The wall of the room faded away until a lush green hillside with small animals and flowers and birds chirping loudly appeared. Patty looked in awe, then turned to the Angel.

"Is this Heaven?"

He smiled, "Yes. God heard the cry of your heart, Patty. He saw no one was going to help you. I am taking you to your new home in Heaven, where you will be young, and strong, and happy forever."

Patty began to cry. "Oh, thank you."

* * * *

As Patty and her Angel disappeared, Rosie and Barbara found themselves alone inside Patty's room. Rosie asked, "Did you learn anything, Barbara?"

"I noticed that Patty's husband was a jerk, and… I was glad that tall man came to visit her. And… her friend Deena was very special."

"But Deena is a drug addict, Barbara. Isn't she pretty low on your totem pole?"

Barbara glared. She knew who she was talking about.

Rosie said, "Friendships are very important to people who are suffering. It gives them hope, often in the darkest of circumstances. Not too long ago, your niece Stephanie spent months in a rehab place about as dismal as this. She became a friend to many of the residents and encouraged them too."

Barbara shook her head and rolled her eyes. "Okay, I get it. Guilty as charged."

Rosie paused, then asked, "When you put your mother in a nursing home, did you ever take the time to visit her? Have you ever taken the time to visit anyone in a nursing home?"

Barbara fumed and turned to face her, enraged at her accusation. "I spent a fortune putting my mother in a first-class nursing home. I paid for *all* of it myself. No one else helped!"

Rosie raised her hand, silencing her. She then raised her arm, and they were back in Barbara's family room, standing in front of her Christmas tree. Barbara decided she was going to hurry up and get this over with. She did not wait to be told, but quickly reached down and picked up the next gift. As soon as she opened it, the room began to spin, and she grabbed hold of Rosie's arm. A date and place appeared in her mind.

December 28ᵗʰ 1833
Bethlehem, Judea
The Fourth Day of Christmas

Barbara and Rosie were in a very old home with stone walls and a thatched roof. A fire was going. It was 1833.

"God, where are we?" Barbara asked, her voice filled with shock.

Rosie whispered, "In Bethlehem. I am personally connected to this story. Watch carefully." Rosie held up her finger to her mouth, signaling silence.

Barbara grimaced and reluctantly turned to watch.

* * * *

Sarah walked over to the fireplace and kissed her husband, Samuel. "I am going now, Samuel. Are you sure you don't want to come with us?"

"No, Sarah. I am too tired from working today."

"But it is the Feast."

"I know, I know. I will keep it here, in my private prayers."

"Very good, my husband," she said as she turned to the back room where her grandchild David was sitting. "David, we are going now. Come and put your sandals on."

In a moment, a spry boy of 9 years old, with thick black hair and dark brown eyes, wearing a white tunic, with a brown belt fastened around his waist, bounded out of the room. "I am ready, Nanna."

TWELVE DAYS • 62

The boy ran to the door and sat on the nearby chair, fastening his brown sandals. Sarah helped him put on a sweater and wrap a scarf around his neck and head. "We have a long walk, David," she said, "I want you to stay warm."

She pulled on her own sweater and headscarf, then took his hand and left out the front door. It was a chilly night in Bethlehem. It reminded Sarah how it must have been on the night when Joseph and Mary came into Bethlehem thousands of years earlier. It might have been just as cold and just as dark as Joseph led Mary on a donkey, down the very same road she and her grandson were walking on.

It was quiet tonight, as the first day of the Great Feast of Christmas had already passed. Still, there were more people coming out within the hour as the Mass of the Holy Innocents was being held at 7 p.m. in the Church of the Nativity. Sarah expected it would be full.

It always was this time of year.

The church had been built by Helena, the mother of Emperor Constantine, in the Fourth Century. It was one of the most beautiful churches in Bethlehem. Sarah's family could trace their roots all the way back to the very first people who attended it. It was a long family line and one which they proudly professed.

Before going to the Church tonight, Sarah had promised to take her grandson to see the cave where Jesus was born. They walked toward the edge of town and then took the road that led to some caves outside the city.

It was a dark, moonless night, and it seemed the stars shined more brightly than normal. Sarah thought that this night must have been like the one Joseph and Mary experienced long ago when they came into Bethlehem with no one or no place to welcome them. She stopped and bent down on one knee, pulling David close, and pointed up to the sky, "Look, David. Look at those stars. Do you see them?"

"I do, Nanna."

"Do you see the one over there, the one that looks the brightest?" She pointed again.

"Yes, I do."

"That star is like the one the shepherds saw long ago. It was an even brighter star that led them here to the outskirts of Bethlehem to find the infant Jesus."

Her grandson looked at the sky, marveling at it. Sarah was happy he appreciated the story. She continued, "The shepherds followed that star from way over there." She pointed into the distance. "They were out there, tending their flocks when the Angel appeared to them, telling them to go to Bethlehem to find the Savior, who had been born into the world. And do you know where they found this baby?"

Her grandson shook his head, "No. Where, Nanna?"

She pointed up to the top of the hillside, "Over there, in a cave on top of that hillside. Come with me. I will show you."

* * * *

They went up the dusty road leading up the hill to the caves where it was thought the traditional Nativity, the place of Jesus' birth, had taken place. They could see clearly into the cave, as it was lit with torches as it always was this time of year for the people who came to see it. Sarah walked in, holding her grandson's hand tightly. She ducked under a beam, and there in front of her was a large Nativity scene. There was a stone carving of Joseph, and Mary, with the infant Jesus in between them, laying on a bed of straw inside a small manger.

"There, right there," Sarah said. "Jesus, Mary, and Joseph were here in this cave, just like the statues show. Isn't it beautiful?"

Her grandson looked around and said, "It is very small, and it is cold in here."

Sarah was grateful her grandson had noticed the dank conditions. She turned to him, "It was like this too, on the night he was born."

David nodded, trying to take it all in. Sarah then took him outside and pointed further up the hillside, past the cave. "David, on the 13th night after the birth of Jesus, Mary and Joseph were warned to flee immediately because King Herod was coming with his soldiers and horses. There were many young boys in Bethlehem at that time, and since King Herod did not know which of them was Jesus, he killed all the young boys under 2 years old." Sarah paused, and quickly made the sign of the cross before continuing, "Jesus, and Mary, and Joseph all escaped just before Herod arrived."

David lowered his head, saddened, then looked out at the village of Bethlehem, thinking. Sarah continued, "David, on that night, the cries and screams of families and young parents could be heard up here. One of our ancestors, a young woman, named Nava, was up here, on this hill. She heard the cries, and she took her sword and ran down this very hill, toward Bethlehem." Sarah pointed down the hillside. "She tried to save anyone she could, and she did save one of them. But right after, she was killed by Herod's soldiers. We remember her to this day for her bravery."

"Nanna, what was her name again?"

Sarah smiled, "Her name was Nava."

"Nava? That is a nice name. Tell me more about her," said her grandson.

"I will, but not now, David. We have to hurry to Church for the service. Tonight, we remember that sorrowful night so long ago. It is called the Feast of the Holy Innocents. Come, let us go."

Sarah pulled her grandson along, down the same road their ancestor Nava had traveled on her way back to the city so long ago.

As they walked, David asked, "Nanna, when will you tell me the story of Nava?"

Sarah smiled, looking down at the boy as they hurried along, and said, "Tomorrow night is the Fifth Day of Christmas. I will tell you the story of Nava after we have dinner and say our family prayers."

"Okay, Nanna. Thank you."

* * * *

The scene faded, and Barbara and Rosie were standing on the hillside road leading out of Bethlehem. Rosie asked, "Did you learn anything?"

"I don't know. It was interesting, I guess, but…"

Rosie asked, "Did you not see the wonder on the young boy's face?"

"Yes, and?" Barbara stopped, not sure of the lesson she was supposed to learn.

Rosie said, "Christmas stories are full of wonder and bravery and miracles. This grandmother went out of her way to tell her grandson about one of these stories, and she brought him out of the house to show him as well."

"I know. I know. I should have agreed to go to Church with my granddaughter, Avery."

Rosie lamented, "That would have meant a lot to her."

"Well, I understand… but… I don't think that Herod killed the Innocents of Bethlehem," she said slowly, trying to back out of her responsibility.

Rosie looked at her, sad at her unwillingness to embrace the magic of Christmas.

Barbara added, lukewarmly, "It was on the History Channel."

"It did happen, Barbara," said Rosie "It all happened just as it has been told. I was here on that night long ago. I was up there on the hillside when nearly a hundred of Herod's soldiers charged in on horseback, carrying swords and torches. I saw what they did. I saw the innocent children, and many of their young parents die. Yes, it really did happen."

Barbara swallowed, mortified. A moment earlier, she had felt vindicated. Now she felt embarrassed. She looked up at Rosie, then out to the distant village and fields, thinking.

Rosie lifted her arm, and they were back in Barbara's family room. Rosie asked, "Are you ready for the Sixth Lesson of Christmas?"

"We are on the Fifth," Barbara said, with her eyebrows furrowed.

Rosie's eyes narrowed, as she scanned the number of remaining gifts, "Oh, yes. You are right. Sorry."

Rosie pointed at the remaining gifts, and Barbara chose the next one. As she opened it, the room began to spin, and she grabbed onto Rosie's arm. A flash of light came, and the date and place appeared in her mind.

December 29th 2020
Cleveland, Ohio
The Fifth Day of Christmas

She and Rosie were in a very modest home in an older neighborhood of Cleveland. Barbara could tell, because the houses were all the same, in size and décor. "Where have you brought me now?" Barbara asked flippantly.

Rosie looked at her crossly, and said, "Just listen!"

* * * *

Jerry's wife, Nina anxiously walked into the kitchen holding a piece of paper from the previous day's mail. "Jerry, we missed our mortgage payment!"

"I know. Don't you think I know!"

"Well, what are we going to do about it?" she asked in a heated tone.

Their youngest, a girl named Abigail, who was 3 years old, started to cry, frightened by the tension in her mother's voice.

"I start at the restaurant tonight! I should have enough money before the late fee date."

"Jerry, what are we going to do? We have four kids. Being a waiter is not going to bring in enough money. How are we going to make the payment next month?"

"Nina, we will make it. I told you the interview today went well." He knew he was lying to her. The interview did not go well. Barbara's firing felt like a major setback in his career. This was his fifth job in less than 10 years. His resume was suddenly throwing up red flags, flags that made employers worry he was a job hopper, or worse, incompetent. None of it was true. It was just circumstance.

"You said that this time it would be different, but you were fired! Again!" Nina said, as she picked up the baby and ran up the stairs to her room, weeping, shouting, "I can't take this stress anymore."

Jerry started to follow her, but his other children, ages 4, 5, and 7, were sitting in the living room with sad looks on their faces. They had been listening. Jerry stopped and sat with them. "Don't worry, kids. Mom is upset, but everything is going to be okay."

Over two years earlier, when he got the job at Barbara's firm, he was sure he had found a place to call home. That was before Barbara turned on him and began harping on him relentlessly. Still, it did not worry him because he knew he was doing the best work of his career. He knew that ultimately the clients were being well served. He only had to win Barbara over, and things would settle down.

Then she fired him.

He hadn't deserved it.

He glanced out the front window and saw the mailman walking up the sidewalk, and he sighed.

More bills.

He waited, then got the mail and rifled through it. "Dammit!"

There was another letter from his bank, and by the looks of it, he already knew it was an overdraft notice. He ripped it open and stared down at it, his eyes watering. He had not expected Barbara to cut him off so quickly. He also had not balanced his checkbook in some time. There was no need to. He had been making plenty of money.

He went down to his office in the basement and called the bank. "Hi, this is Jerry Tracek. I just got a notice of two overdraft charges. I have to ask that these be reversed."

"Just a moment," said the assistant manager. "Let me pull up your account."

There was silence for a moment.

"I am sorry, Mr. Tracek. We just reversed a charge for you last month. We cannot do another."

"Listen to me, please!" he shouted. "I cannot afford this right now."

Again, there was silence.

Jerry lamented, "Can you at least reverse one?"

"I will have to ask my manager," the assistant said.

"Thank you," Jerry said in an exasperated tone.

He heard the on-hold music for several minutes. Then the assistant picked up. "Mr. Tracek?"

"Yes?"

"I'm sorry. My manager said there is nothing we can do."

"Dammit! I am pulling my account from there!"

"You can do that, sir. I *AM* sorry. Is there anything else?"

"No!" Jerry shouted, slamming down the phone.

"Who was that?" Nina asked in a worried tone from the top of the steps.

"No one!" Jerry said. "Look, just... just leave me alone... please, Nina."

She slammed the door leading to the basement.

Jerry buried his head in his hands and looked up at the clock. It was 1:30 p.m. He had to be at the restaurant at 4 p.m. He dreaded having to go. He had a college degree and an MBA, and now he would be waiting tables. While he dreaded it, he was happy to do whatever it took to get his family out of this hole.

* * * *

Barbara suddenly felt the wind in her hair and in an instant she and Rosie were standing in a quaint, crowded and loud restaurant in a place called Little Italy, a bustling ethnic neighborhood a few miles from Jerry's home.

"Wait, what are we doing here? I've already seen enough."

"I am not sure you have seen enough. Watch."

* * * *

Jerry walked past, anxiously following a waitress. It appeared she had been training him. A manager called him aside. "Jerry, normally I let training go the whole night, but we are slammed. Are you ready to take a few tables?"

"Yes, ma'am," Jerry replied.

"Alright. Start with that couple over there."

Jerry smiled and went to work. By the end of their meal, the couple left him a $15 dollar tip. Right after, the manager called out, "Jerry, take table 25."

"Yes, ma'am," Jerry said.

Jerry turned the page in his order book and walked over, cheerfully saying, "Good evening, welcome to La Dolce Vita. May I start you off with something to drink?"

The man lowered the menu and looked up at him. "Yes, get us... Jerry?"

Jerry felt his entire being sink. It was Steve Garrity, of Loktite Corp.

"Mr. Garrity, good evening."

"What are you doing here?" Steve asked.

"Oh.... Just... you know, picking up some extra money... for Christmas bills."

Steve Garrity looked across the table at his associate, "Jim, this is Jerry Tracek, from Barbara DiSanto's company. He is working on our account."

"Hi, Jerry. It is nice to meet you."

"So what?" Steve asked, "Isn't Barbara paying you enough?"

"Actually, I don't work for her anymore."

"Oh, what happened?"

"Ummm… to be honest, she fired me."

Steve paused, "I'm sorry. I didn't know. Well, I hope you land on your feet." Steve glanced back at the menu, then looked up, asking, "Why did she fire you?"

"I don't really know. But… I… wish her the best. She is very good at what she does."

"Well, that's very noble of you."

Jerry changed the subject. "Well, enough about me, what can I get you?"

The men proceeded to order. Jerry got them their drinks, then took their food order. He put it into the kitchen and went out back.

It was dark outside, and the place where the servers gathered to talk and smoke when they could, was empty. He walked further into the alley to make sure he would be alone. He hit his fist against the building, trying to stop the tears attempting to eke out of the corners of his eyes. He felt so humiliated seeing Mr. Garrity.

Just then the 7 p.m. bells from Holy Rosary Church down the street began to ring. Jerry looked up, wiping his eyes dry. It was starting to snow, and he felt peace he did not understand. He gathered his courage, put a half-smile on his face, and went back in.

* * * *

Rosie and Barbara stood in the alley watching him. Rosie looked over at Barbara, surprised to see the cross look on her face.

"What's wrong, Barbara?"

"He just almost cost me my biggest account. That's what wrong!"

"You have no more accounts," Rosie said softly.

Barbara turned away, and looked into the restaurant, with an angry look on her face.

Rosie shook her head, "Barbara, don't you get it? You suddenly fired him at Christmas, and still, he did not speak ill of you."

Barbara lifted her eyes with gritted teeth. "He deserved to be fired."

"I don't agree with you, but may I ask about your promise?"

"What promise?"

"You promised to give each other a month's notice. You did not honor your promise. Instead, you cut the legs out from under that poor family, and it left Jerry very shaken. Doesn't that bother you?"

Barbara turned to her, and smugly said, "You know, Rosie, like I told my husband, my business affairs are none of your business. I fired him because I wanted to, and I would do it again!"

Rosie lowered her glance to the ground. "Oh, Barbara," she said in a pleading tone, "I wish you understood. Oh, how I wish you understood."

"Understood what?" Barbara demanded.

"That the way you treat people *is* my business, and unfortunately, it *is* your business too, more than you realize."

Barbara swallowed hard. Rosie's tone scared her, and her words scared her even more. Using the word 'business' had gotten her attention. Rosie meant business. A sinking feeling took hold of her.

Rosie wiped the tear from the corner of her eye and raised her hand into the air, and they were in her family room before the Christmas tree.

She pointed to the remaining gifts. Barbara frowned, still shaken by Rosie's words. She reached down, picked up the next gift, and opened it. The room began to spin, and she closed her eyes. She wanted to scream 'stop.' She wanted to get off this merry-go-round and return to her business and her life. But the light flashed, and a date and place appeared in her mind.

December 30th 1943
Celle, Germany
The Sixth Day of Christmas

Suddenly, she and Rosie were in a chilly bedroom, standing before a sleeping older couple. The smell of the room was clean and simple, like Barbara remembered her old grandmother's house being.

Barbara exclaimed, "Why am I in Germany in the middle of a war?"

Rosie glanced over at her, and said, "You will see."

* * * *

Klaus heard a noise coming from the alley. He looked over at his wife, Frieda. She was sound asleep. He swung his feet quietly out of bed and sat in the silence for a moment, listening. There was another noise. Someone was in the alley behind his home and bakery.

He put his slippers on and got up, careful not to wake his wife. He reached up to the shelf and got the pistol his son Rolf had given him. He went down the hall, through the living room, and over to the window by the Christmas tree. From there, he would be able to see down into the alley.

There was someone there all right, but the moon was new tonight, so it was too dark to make out who. Klaus went down the narrow stairs that led from their upstairs living quarters into the back of his bakery, which occupied the first floor. Whoever was out there was going through a small garbage can just outside the back door. He went to the door and peered out through the small window. It looked to be a woman, but he could not be sure. She had her back to him. Her head was wrapped tightly in a thick woolen scarf, and she had no coat. Her shoes were flimsy, not the sturdy kind someone would be wearing in the middle of winter.

Klaus carefully turned the doorknob and opened the door. The woman was 10 feet away from him, bent over, looking through the garbage. Klaus stepped outside and crept up, then grabbed her around the neck with one arm, thrusting the gun into her side with the other. "Don't move, or I will shoot you."

The woman did not cry out but seemed to exhale only exhaustion. Klaus could feel her weakness in the lack of resistance. He pulled her back into the house, then put the gun under her chin, forcing her to stand against the wall.

"Who are you?" he asked.

"I am just a beggar looking for food."

"Why are you a beggar? You... you don't sound German. Are you a spy?" he asked, pressing the gun further into her skin.

"No, please. I am with child, and I am hungry."

"Are you a spy?" he demanded.

"Klaus? Who are you talking to?" It was his wife, Frieda, calling from the top of the stairs.

"Come down, Frieda," he said, holding the gun and the woman firmly against the wall.

The light of a lamp came around the corner, followed by Frieda. As she neared the back of the shop, she stopped. "What is going on, Klaus?" She stepped closer, holding up the lamp, giving light to them all.

For the first time, Klaus could see the woman clearly. Her face was gaunt as if she had not eaten in weeks. She was not lying about being hungry. Her hair was brown but very short, almost not there, as if it had been shaved off some time ago and only grown partially back. Her clothing consisted of a blue blouse and an oversized black wool skirt. Her shoes were brown and seemed too big for the bare feet they housed.

Frieda held the lamp to her face, then lowered it to her midsection. "She is with child, Klaus."

"I know. That is what she said."

"Are you a Jew?" Frieda asked with suspicion in her tone.

The woman closed her tired, hungry eyes and nodded.

No one said a word as the reality of the situation descended upon them all.

Klaus said, "We must turn her in."

"No," the woman pleaded, her eyes revealing the horror she felt at hearing this. "They will take me back and kill me." She looked down, then up at Frieda, pleading, "I want my baby to live."

"Where did you come from?" Klaus asked.

"From the Star Camp, the women's camp at Bergen Belden."

Klaus's eyes widened. Their son, Rolf, was the commandant of the camp. Rolf was a prominent member of the Nazi Party, having attained the distinction and rank of Hauptsturmführer, the equivalent of Captain in the feared SS. He had been in charge of the entire camp since that spring. All that Klaus and Frieda knew was that the camp was used for prisoners of war. There had been rumors that Jews were being sent there too, but according to their son, only Jews who were plotting against the Fatherland from within were being arrested. They had to be arrested, he had insisted, but he had told them they would all be released after the war was won.

The woman interrupted his thoughts, "Please don't send me back there. They will kill me." Her eyes held the desperation of her plea.

Frieda held the lamp to the woman's face again, then leaned back and whispered into Klaus' ear. "Let us take her upstairs, Klaus. We will give her some food and question her further in the morning."

"No, Frieda. We cannot help her."

Frieda leaned forward, whispering again, "Klaus, please. She is desperate. She needs to eat."

He nodded, then lowered the gun from her chin. "Go up the stairs," he said, waving it, pointing her toward the stairs, "But you leave in the morning."

* * * *

They went up the stairs and to the back of the parlor, where another staircase led to an attic. Klaus opened the door and waved the gun, pointing for her to go up the dark wooden stairs.

The attic was dark and cold. The roofline slanted down both sides from a narrow stretch along the peak that was just tall enough to stand in. The floor was made of old thick dark oak boards. Klaus pointed to a corner and said, "Sit there. We will bring you some food."

The woman sat, and Frieda went downstairs as Klaus guarded the door. A few minutes later, she returned with a plate containing an apple, a piece of bread, and a small piece of sausage. She handed it to the woman, who took it, and stared at it for a moment, then looked up, with a tear rolling down her face, and said, "Thank you."

"Go ahead," Frieda said. "Eat."

The woman did not wait but immediately began eating. Frieda motioned to Klaus that they should leave. They went downstairs and closed the door.

* * * *

Frieda paced nervously in the front room. She asked, "What are we going to do, Klaus?"

He replied, "We have to tell Rolf."

Frieda's eyes widened, "No!" she exclaimed. "Not until we find out more."

"Find out what? She is a Jew and an enemy of the Fatherland. We cannot be caught with her. It will shame us and shame our son."

Frieda's eyes narrowed with worry, "I have heard rumors about the camp, rumors I did not want to believe. We can ask her about them. If she is lying, we will turn her over to Rolf. He will be here in two days."

"No," said Klaus, "We must send word to him now."

"Klaus, but... what if she is telling the truth? We cannot send her to her death. And what about the baby?"

Klaus angrily replied, "It is none of our concern, Frieda!" He glanced up and said in a hushed tone, "If she is an enemy of the Fatherland, she must go back. That is why our son is the commandant, to protect us from them."

Frieda turned, shaking her head, "We will talk more later. I will get her a blanket." Frieda got a blanket, a pillow, and a small chamber pot and brought it upstairs. She gave it to the woman and asked, "What is your name?"

The woman looked up slowly, and in a weak voice, said, "My name is Alma."

"Who is the commandant of your camp?" Frieda asked, testing her. The woman's countenance fell, and she swallowed, "His name is Commandant Rolf Schmidt."

"Why do you say that you will be killed?"

"He has sent thousands to their deaths. My own sister was one of them." The woman began to cry.

"But what did she do?" Frieda asked, adding, "She must have done something?"

Alma slowly shook her head. "Our only crime is being Jewish."

"How did you escape?"

"I was able to escape from the brothel. Once my sister died, I was chosen to take her place."

Frieda stepped back, her eyes narrowed, "You are a whore?"

"You don't understand. If I had not gone into the brothel, I would have surely died. Only by going there was I able to survive."

Frieda shook her head, "I don't believe you."

Alma said, "Maybe you will believe this." She opened her blouse. On her chest was a crude tattoo. It read "Field Whore."

Alma allowed her to look at it as another tear fell down her face. "Do you think I would do this to myself? The commandant himself ordered that all women in the brothel be given this mark." Alma lowered her head, and with shaking hands, quickly buttoned her blouse, "My sister had this mark too when they carried her body to the crematorium."

"To what?" Frieda asked, her tone filled with outraged skepticism.

Alma replied, staring blankly ahead, unable to look at Frieda, "It is true. When anyone dies, they take them to a building where their bodies are burned. The ovens run day and night." Her voice trailed off as her eyes glanced to the window, "So many dead… my own sister burned up like a piece of wood." She began to choke back tears.

Frieda turned away. *It is impossible. She is tricking me. She must know who I am. The rumors. What if the rumors are true? This woman is… is… is telling the truth. But she might be tricking me.* Frieda turned back, and snapped, "No, I don't believe you."

Alma said nothing for several moments, then said, "I am sorry to have told you all this. But I swear, it is true."

Frieda turned her head slightly, not willing to look into the eyes of the woman sitting in front of her, not willing to face what might very well be true. "Sleep here. In the morning, you can empty your chamber pot and take a bath. I have some clean clothes for you."

"Thank you," Alma said, looking up with her eyes, hoping to show her sincerity.

Frieda started away, then stopped, "When is your baby due?"

Alma looked down at her stomach, with her eyes filled with cautious hope, and said, "I don't know, but I feel it could be very soon."

Frieda sighed and went downstairs and bolted the door. She went to her room, where Klaus was waiting.

He asked, "Did you speak to her?"

"Yes."

"What did she say?"

Frieda could not tell him yet. She needed to process it. "We will talk in the morning."

"Did you bolt the door?" he asked.

"Yes, I did."

"Goodnight," Klaus said as he rolled over and went to sleep.

Frieda laid awake thinking. *The rumors must be true. Here is a witness. Alma is not the kind of woman who would lie about such a thing.* But, what about Rolf, her dear and wonderful son, Rolf. He was so strong and brave. He would never harm....

She stopped.

Rolf had changed.

He never hid his true beliefs, his 'Nazi' beliefs. Everyone had to profess their belief in the Nazi party. Because of their son's rise in the ranks, even her husband Klaus became caught up with the Nazi's, and though she privately did not, she wondered at times how far Klaus might go, but Rolf was a very different story. There was no question where his loyalty lay.

He had started out as one of the Hitler Youth. Ever since that time, her little boy had been gradually slipping from her grasp. Now, he was an important officer, in charge of the entire POW camp system at Bergen Belden, only 30 miles to the north of Celle.

She and Klaus were treated very special by all the townspeople because their son held such a position of honor and great responsibility. Was it a position of great atrocities too? No, she would not believe it. Not until she confronted Rolf and asked him herself.

But what to do with Alma? She was about to have her baby. And Rolf was coming to visit them in two days to celebrate a Christmas meal. What if Klaus turned her in?

She stopped again.

She and Klaus would either get her out before then or make certain she was silent. She would discuss it all in the morning with Klaus.

She needed to be sure he would cooperate, or she would send Alma back into the cold night to fend for herself.

As bad as it seemed, at least she would have a chance to find help.

* * * *

The following morning Frieda sat with Klaus and told him all that Alma had told her.

Klaus was not so easily convinced. "I am sure she knows the same rumors we do, Frieda. She could be lying to us."

"We need to be sure," Frieda demanded, though agreeing with him.

Klaus said, "What if Rolf finds her here? How will we explain it? We cannot!"

Frieda thought about what he said. "You are right. Tonight, when it is dark, I will send her away."

"No," Klaus said, saying adamantly, "We need to turn her in. I have already written to Rolf asking him to come early tomorrow."

"What! How could you?" Frieda said, standing abruptly. "Did you tell him?"

"No, I did not, but he must know! We cannot hide something like this from him."

Frieda vowed right then that she would turn Alma out as soon as Klaus went to bed.

That evening, Frieda brought a dish of food upstairs to Alma, who had been locked in the attic all day. She saw that she was asleep. She bent down and asked, "How are you feeling?"

Alma raised her head slightly and shook it slowly, "I don't feel good. I am having some pains."

"What kind of pains?" Frieda asked, alarmed.

Alma put her hands on her stomach, wincing, "Birth pains."

"How often?" Frieda asked, suddenly not sure if Rolf coming earlier was a good thing or a bad thing.

"Not that often. Every couple of hours."

Frieda knew what this meant. The baby would be coming soon, perhaps within mere days. She touched Alma's arm and said, "I will be back to check on you. Eat this food and go to sleep."

Frieda checked on her a few hours later, bringing her something to drink and some more food. She asked about the labor pains, but they were the same. "I will be back later tonight, Alma."

As Frieda turned to leave, Alma whispered faintly, "Frieda, what is going to happen to me? Are you going to turn me in?"

Frieda shook her head, "No, I won't let that happen to you."

"But what about your husband? He does not seem as kind as you."

Frieda turned back to her, "I said, I won't let that happen to you. Now go to sleep."

Frieda was worried. She could not rightly send a woman about to give birth into the streets; yet her son was coming.

She needed to convince Klaus.

After supper, they lit their Christmas tree, and Klaus sat at the piano, playing Christmas songs. When he played Silent Night, Frieda came over and sat next to him and hummed along.

They heard a cough.

Klaus got up and went to the attic door, thrusting it open. Alma was sitting on the step with her hands folded. "What are you doing?" Klaus demanded.

"I was listening to the song."

"What would that song mean to you?" he asked scoffingly.

"My grandmother was a Gentile. She used to sing Silent Night to me."

Frieda came over, "It is all right, Klaus. It is Christmastime. Let the girl be."

She took Alma by the hand and said, "Come and listen with us."

Alma walked her to the couch, and they sat together. Alma was stiff and scared, afraid she had angered Klaus. But Frieda put her arm around her and said, "It's okay, Alma." She motioned to Klaus and said gently, "Klaus, play Silent Night for us."

Klaus reluctantly sat at the piano bench and started to play.

Frieda clutched Alma's trembling hand and began to sing.

Silent night, holy night
All is calm, all is bright
Round yon virgin, mother and child
Holy infant, so tender and mild
Sleep in heavenly peace
Sleep, sleep in heaven, heavenly peace

Silent night, holy night
Shepherds quake at the sight
Glories streams from heaven afar
Heavenly hosts sing, alleluia
Christ, the savior is born.
Christ, the savior is born

Frieda kept humming along and signaled for Klaus to keep playing. Alma sat with tears in her eyes, clutching Frieda's hand. For a moment, she dozed off, then suddenly woke with a startled, scared look on her face.

"It's okay," Frieda said, "Close your eyes. You are safe here."

After some time of quiet sitting, Alma said, "Thank you, both. This night, this song has meant more to me than you will ever know." She got up and went back up into the attic.

Later that night, Frieda called Klaus into the bedroom and closed the door. She said, "Klaus, Rolf is coming in the morning. We cannot tell him. I believe the girl."

Klaus cut her off, "No, Frieda. Rolf would never do those things. If he did, it would be to our enemies only."

"But what if all the rumors are true?" she cried, her eyes pleading for him to see at least the possibility.

"Our Rolf is no murderer, Frieda."

Frieda grabbed him by the shirt sleeves. "Klaus, don't you understand. If the rumors are true, and if Rolf is ordering these people to their deaths, he is not a murderer. He is a monster!"

Klaus knocked her hands off his arms and turned, "I don't believe it."

She grabbed him again, "You must consider it, Klaus."

He turned away and went out into the living room. Frieda followed him and sat down in front of the Christmas tree. She did the only thing left she could do. She prayed.

*   *   *   *

After Klaus went to bed, Frieda went to the kitchen and prepared a sack of food. Alma would be safer leaving. She would have to depend on someone else. Klaus was not going to keep quiet. She went upstairs. Alma was lying on her side, quietly moaning. "What is wrong?" Frieda asked.

"The pains are more often, and my lower back hurts."

"How often?"

"I had several tonight," she said, barely able to respond due to the pain she was experiencing.

Frieda held a sack in her hand filled with food, then set it down. "Here, eat some of this food. Make it last. You will need it. I cannot come up here tomorrow morning. You must be absolutely silent. Do you understand? My son will be here, and he works at the camp you said you are from."

Alma's eyes widened, "I have to get out of here!"

"No, you can't. The baby is coming soon. He will only be here for an hour or so. You must keep silent."

"I will," Alma said.

* * * *

The following morning, Frieda nervously waited. Then, she heard the car pull up out front, and orders shouted, and car doors opened and shut. Next came the sound of soldiers coming swiftly up the steps. The door opened, and there was Rolf.

"Good morning, Mother and Father," Rolf said as he walked in their upstairs apartment door. He stood straight and tall, wearing his neatly polished black SS uniform, shiny black boots, and black Captain's hat. He hugged Frieda tightly, "I have missed you, Mother. Merry Christmas to you. I have gifts." He turned to the hall, and a soldier walked in carrying several boxes neatly wrapped.

"Oh, thank you," Frieda said, trying to appear happy. In truth, she was petrified.

"Put them down," Rolf snapped at the soldier, "Wait for me in the car."

"Yavole!" snapped the young soldier as he turned and walked out.

With a wide smile on his face, Rolf turned, "Father, Merry Christmas to you."

Frieda's heart dropped as Klaus opened his mouth for the first time, saying, "Merry Christmas, my son. We are so proud of you."

Rolf walked in, strutting across the modest living room. He looked down at his waiting staff car, with its open top and mounted flags of the Reich billowing in the late December wind. He was happy his parents held such an esteemed place because of his high rank. He turned and sat on the couch, putting his shiny black boots up on the coffee table. "So, how is everything here?"

Klaus followed him in and sat down. Frieda stood silently in the kitchen, listening and praying.

Klaus replied, "We are doing well, son. How… how is going at the camp?"

"Oh, you know. We are taking care of business."

"It must be hard with all those prisoners."

Rolf's eyes narrowed, and his face grew cross, "No, it is not hard at all. They obey the rules, and they are fine. If they don't, they are punished. It is straightforward, Father. It is the way our Fuhrer wants it to be."

Frieda came out of the kitchen, passing by the closed attic door, carrying a plate of eggs and sausages and another one with sliced toast. She set them down on the preset dining room table. Frieda desperately wanted to get on with the meal. "Come to the table, Rolf and Klaus. The meal is ready."

They ate quietly, with Rolf commenting on how delicious their food was. "I miss your cooking, Mother."

Frieda returned the comment with only a smile, hoping to hide her growing nervousness. She dished out the food and sat at the table. They bowed their heads for a moment of silence, then began to eat.

When they finished eating, Rolf said, "Father, play some Christmas songs for me before I go."

Frieda felt her breath leap within her. He was leaving soon, and so far, Klaus had not said anything.

Rolf turned in his chair and watched his father sit on the bench. He played Silent Night. Then, he played The First Noel. Rolf sang along with the both of them. Then, he played God Rest Ye Merry Gentlemen. When he was done, Rolf said, "It is a beautiful time for all of us Christians. Thank you, Father."

Klaus turned and cleared his throat. "I wanted to talk with you about something, son."

Frieda got up and picked up a plate. She went to stand by the attic door, not knowing what she would do, only knowing she had to do something.

Suddenly a siren began blaring. Several cars screeched to a stop out front. Rolf stood up and went to the window. The sound of men running up the steps could be heard. Frieda watched the look on Rolf's face. It had turned very angry looking, but an anger possessing command and authority.

It scared her.

There was a loud pounding on the door. "Come in!" Rolf shouted. Suddenly, Frieda heard a gasp come from the attic door behind her. Rolf turned, and Frieda dropped her plate, letting it shatter on the tile floor. "I am sorry!" she yelled, "I was startled."

Rolf turned to the soldier, "What is it!"

"Two prisoners have escaped, Commandant!"

Rolf's eyes narrowed. He picked up his hat and grabbed his overcoat. "Move!" he shouted. He led the way past the soldier and down the stairs. Frieda ran to the window, followed by Klaus.

Even though he was outside, they could hear Rolf. Another officer was standing in the street at attention, waiting for him. "How did this happen!" Rolf shouted with a voice as angry and sinister as Frieda had ever heard.

"We don't know, Heir Commandant!"

"You know what to do!" Rolf shouted. "Round up 20 prisoners and put them in the starvation bunker!"

"Yavole, Heir Commandant," snapped the officer.

"Snell!" shouted Rolf. The officer turned and ran to his car, and they sped off. Rolf slapped his gloves against his waiting car, then turned and came marching up the stairs.

He walked in, glancing at the attic door, then glancing down at the shattered plate. He smiled as if nothing had happened. "I am sorry to have startled you both, Mother and Father. What did you want to tell me, Father?"

Frieda wanted to cry. She thought they were saved with him leaving, and now it was all over. Klaus was going to tell everything.

Klaus said, "Nothing, Rolf. Nothing important. Go, and take care... of your business."

Rolf snapped to attention, turned, and left.

Frieda went to the couch, too overcome with emotion to stand or think. She started to cry. Klaus went to his room and shut the door.

After a while, Frieda went upstairs into the attic. Alma was lying on her side. Frieda asked, "How are you?"

"I think the baby is coming soon," Alma said, barely able to speak.

"I will help you," Frieda said.

Alma said, "I am sorry that I gasped. That man... he... he..."

"He is my son Rolf." Frieda lowered her head, "He is the Commandant."

Alma said in a mournful tone, "Yes, I have seen him."

"Where?"

Alma began to cry, saying, "He came to the brothel a lot when I first got there."

"Did he ever touch you?"

"Y... y... yes... " Alma lowered her eyes in shame.

Frieda took hold of her, hugging her warmly, "It's okay, Alma. You did nothing wrong."

Alma cried.

Frieda asked in a trembling voice, "Is... is he the father of the baby?"

Alma froze, then shook her head, "I cannot be sure. There were so many."

She hoped her lie was believable. Like her sister, she had become the Commandant's favorite. Yes, it was true that she was not sure, but there was a very good chance.

Frieda pulled her closer, nestling her in her arms, "My poor, poor girl. I will help you. I don't know how, but we will find a way to get you across the border."

Alma looked up, her eyes wet with tears, "Thank you, Frieda. I am going to name my daughter Sara, but I want Frieda to be her middle name to honor you for all you have done."

Frieda cradled her tightly, silently whispering a prayer in her heart to God, thanking him for this miracle, grateful she had found the courage to help.

* * * *

The scene faded into faint mist. Barbara stood silent, stunned at the horror. She turned to Rosie and asked, "What happened to her? Did she make it out of Germany?"

Rosie wiped a tear from the corner of her eye and shook her head. "She made it out and her child lived. They made it to America and Alma passed away from old age a few years ago."

Barbara looked into the mist again but was silent. "Where is the daughter now?"

"She lives in America. She has three children, including a daughter named Alma."

Rosie was quiet, then said, "Sometimes we have to use whatever means we can to help those in need, even complete strangers. It takes courage to stand against what is wrong."

Barbara thought back to the homeless woman she passed nightly and the other homeless woman who looked pregnant and was being attacked outside her parking garage. She lowered her glance feeling a sense of shame.

Rosie raised her hand, and they were back in her family room in front of the Christmas tree. She pointed to the remaining six gifts and said, "Choose the next gift, Barbara."

Barbara reached down, then stopped. "Look, I get it, Rosie. I can be a better person."

"Yes, you could have, and it would have helped so very many."

"Let's just cut to the chase. I am tired of all this."

Rosie shook her head and pointed. "There are six more lessons, Barbara. The powers on high have decreed you see all twelve."

Barbara desperately wanted to pause, still shaken at being confronted with the evils of the Nazi regime, but there was no time. She picked up the next gift and opened it. The room began to spin. She grabbed hold of Rosie's arm.

Just as before, a date and place appeared in her mind.

December 31st 1987
Columbus, Ohio
The Seventh Day of Christmas

Suddenly they were standing in the corner of an out of style, dimly lit apartment bedroom. Barbara tensed up. She recognized this place. She glanced at Rosie. Rosie nodded and Barbara looked back onto the scene.

~ ~ ~ ~

It was early morning on the last day of the year in Columbus, Ohio. Judy lay awake in her room thinking about the dance tonight. She had been up all night trying to get her courage up. *I wish I had as much confidence as Barbara.* She glanced over to her closet. The door was shut, but she knew nothing inside would help her feel better about herself.

Two weeks earlier, she and Barbara had been walking down High Street together on the way to their off-campus apartment on 13th Street. They had just finished taking the final exam in their Business Ethics class, their last final of the semester.

"Oh, look at this," Barbara said enthusiastically as she stepped up to a sign posted on a telephone pole.

"What is it?" asked Judy.

"There is a dance coming up."

Judy stepped up next to Barbara. The words 'dance' sent a slight tinge of fear through her. She read the sign.

New Year's Eve Dance Party
8:00 p.m. to 1:00 a.m.

Drury Hotel and Convention Center

88 E. Nationwide Blvd.

$10 per person.

Barbara turned to her, "We should go?"

"I don't know, Barbara. I feel so out of shape. I don't think… besides, I don't have anything to wear."

"Nonsense," said Barbara. "You look great.

Judy blushed, "Aww, Barbara. You always make me feel good." Judy was quite conscious that the was more than a little round around the edges. She did not feel like she looked great in any respect. But she felt lucky to have Barbara for a roommate.

They had met the previous year in a marketing class. Judy's roommate was graduating, and she had plenty of space. Barbara came over one day, loved the location, and when the next semester started, Barbara left her dorm and moved into Apartment Y, on 13th Street, right near campus.

Barbara was in a different class than her. She had a big family and caring parents and grandparents, firmly established as a middle-class family up in Cleveland. They were not rich, but they got by just fine.

Judy, on the other hand, was the only daughter of Italian immigrants. Her father had been disabled years earlier, and her mother had never held a job outside the home. They were pretty poor but managed to get by and hold their heads up high. It didn't matter. They were both gone now.

Judy was from Cleveland, too. She never met Barbara while she was there. She never met many people, for that matter, leading a somewhat secluded life. Once Barbara decided to move in as her roommate, Judy imagined being helped out of her shell by the outgoing and ever-energetic Barbara. But they were already halfway through the school year. One more semester was all she had left, and so far, despite her desire to do so, she was not getting very far out of her shell.

Barbara wrote down the information from the sign on a piece of paper and said, "Hey, let's grab something to eat."

They walked a few blocks up and went into Athens Gyro shop.

"Ah, good morning, Barbara," said the owner, an immigrant from Greece.

"Good morning, Dimitri. I will have a gyro."

"And how about you, Judy?" Dimitri asked.

"I... I... " she paused, then said, "I will have a Greek salad."

"Oh, a salad. Eating healthy today?" Dimitri asked.

"Yes, I am!" Judy said proudly.

As Dimitri turned to make the food, Judy said, "I'm going to lose these extra pounds this year, and I am *not* waiting for a New Year's resolution to start."

Barbara turned to her, smiling. "That's great, Judy. Does this mean that you want to go to the dance?"

"I am thinking about it." Judy's face tightened some, "I just don't know if I have anything to wear."

"You have some dresses."

"None of them really fit."

This meant the ball was in Judy's court.

That was a week ago, and that was before Mark Kennedy, a finance major from Indianapolis, called and invited Barbara to go to the dance with him. Barbara had met him a few weeks earlier when she and Judy were having lunch in the commons behind the student center.

Now it was the morning of the dance, and Judy felt divided. She glanced over at her closet. The maroon dress was still front and center, staring at her. She had tried it on right after they returned home from the restaurant a week earlier. It didn't fit then, and despite her attempt to eat healthier this week, it didn't fit now.

Judy got up and saw Barbara was still asleep in her room. She quietly made some breakfast and thought long and hard about the dance. She wanted to be there in the worst way, and she kept trying to imagine herself there, in a dress, twirling about, smiling at some of the young men. She was sure they would ask her to dance. She was sure they would like her once they got to know her. But then, she imagined herself looking too heavy, out of balance. She imagined herself feeling ashamed that she was overweight. She went back to bed.

The day progressed slowly. There was not much to do. Barbara was gone most of the day. Where? Judy did not know.

It was near dinner time when Barbara returned to the apartment. Judy was in her room reading when she heard the door open. "Hey, Barbara," she called out.

"Hey, Judy," Barbara replied.

Judy heard her walk straight to her room. Then she heard the door close. After a while, she went into the living room. Barbara was still in her room. "Barbara, do you want me to order some pizza?"

"Sure, that would be fine. Make it a small and get me a salad."

"A salad, yes," Judy said to herself, glancing down at the roll in her midsection. "I will get a salad, too."

The pizza came, and they sat down in the living room together, watching some of the 'Year in Remembrance' shows that play every New Year's Eve.

"So, where were you all day?"

"Oh, I just did a little shopping."

"Oh, that's nice. What for?"

"Just a little bit of clothes."

"I see."

Barbara did not elaborate, and Judy found it strange. She usually did elaborate on things like shopping, often showing Judy everything she bought.

After eating, Barbara said, "I have to get ready." She turned, "Are you sure you don't want to come?"

Judy's heart leaped a bit inside her. She only needed to say yes. The rest would work itself out. But she thought of her dress again and her fear she would look heavy in it. She offered a fake smile and said, "I don't think so."

Barbara smiled robotically and went to her room. A half-hour later, she came back in a beautiful black dress with black sheer hose and black heels. She had on a gold necklace Judy had never seen.

"Oh, Barbara, you look amazing!"

Barbara smiled widely and twirled around. "Do you like it?"

"I love it!"

"Where did you get it?"

"I bought it at a dress shop on High Street today."

Judy felt her heart drop some. She wished she had thought of getting a different dress. She didn't think that way because she didn't have any extra money. She was barely affording groceries and incidentals now that her parents were gone.

Barbara looked at the clock. "Oh, it's almost time. Mark will be here soon. Judy, why don't you get dressed and come with us."

"No, I don't really have anything to wear."

"All right." The horn outside beeped, and Barbara said, "Well, it's time to go. I'll see you later."

Barbara put on her new matching shawl and left.

Judy went back to the living room and picked up the remnants of her salad. She stared at it for a while, then went to the garbage in the kitchen and dumped it out. She turned off the TV, went to her room, and got under the covers. She prayed and prayed and then began to cry, finally falling asleep.

* * * *

Rosie waved her hand, and they were standing in a cloud-like mist. Barbara felt ashamed, but she kept her facial expression fixed, pretending to be unmoved. She could not let Rosie see she was taking responsibility. Whatever fate was coming, she needed to maintain her bargaining position. Showing weakness would thwart her plan. She looked up at Rosie and could see the disappointment on her face.

"What's wrong?" Barbara asked. "It's not my fault she was heavy."

Rosie's face grew somber. "Don't you remember Barbara? Don't you remember when you bought that dress?"

"How am I supposed to remember that?"

"You had just received $50 in a Christmas card your Nanna mailed you. The card read, 'Buy yourself something nice for the New Year. Love, Nanna.'"

"And that's what I did!" Barbara said indignantly.

"Oh, yes, I know. Remember how you saw that dress you thought would look perfect on Judy. Remember, you found another that would look good on you, too. You were all ready to buy those two dresses. You knew Judy would be so surprised. You knew she would love it. You knew it would look great on her. Remember that?"

"I guess, sort of."

"Then you saw that black dress, that very expensive black dress. You found shoes to match and a gold necklace, and by the time you were done, you realized you did not have enough money to help Judy."

"So what?"

"So? You left Judy behind! Did you know the spirit of hope left her that night? Did you know it was a turning point for her?"

"This is too much for me, Rosie. You can't blame me for all the world's problems!"

"Not all the world's problems, Barbara, just the ones you could have done something about."

Barbara said nothing. Her selfishness was suddenly on full display, and it was starting to undo her defenses. She subtly shook her head, trying to deflect the uncomfortable feeling of Rosie looking at her, and sheepishly muttered, "Judy has to live her own life."

Rosie raised her head giving one final measure of observation, then lifted her hand. They faded into Barbara's family room and were in front of the Christmas tree, looking down at the five remaining gifts.

Barbara swallowed. Her interior resistance was fading, but she needed to stay strong on the outside, or else she would have no bargaining position when it would matter most. She reached down somberly, trying not to show the turmoil inside. She chose the next gift. The room began to spin, and she grasped Rosie's arm, then the date and place flashed into her mind.

January 1st 2012
Minneapolis, Minnesota
The Eighth Day of Christmas

Suddenly, she and Rosie were standing at the back of an office. It was a large office, filled with neatly clipped piles of papers. There were plaques and pictures and framed degrees on the wall. An older man, wearing a black shirt and black pants, perhaps late middle age, sat at the desk, alone thinking. Barbara shrugged her shoulders and lifted her hands, looking to Rosie questioningly. Rosie subtly nodded and motioned for her to watch.

* * * *

Father Mark sat quietly in his office, thinking about the parishioners who had come to Mass this morning. It was a Monday, New Year's Day, and an important Feast Day for the Church, the Feast of Mary. It had been celebrated for centuries, going back to the year 431. He was disappointed that there were no more than a handful of people in attendance. The people who even bothered to come to the Church anymore had been there yesterday for Sunday Mass. Turning around and coming back the next day in the cold Minneapolis weather required a certain level of commitment few possessed anymore.

It had always been important to his family.

While he was growing up, no matter the weather, his mother would gather her four children every New Year's Day and bring them to Church. Afterward, they would take a drive to the cemetery to visit his father's grave.

His father had died when he was only 6 years old. Mark's memories of him were faint. His name was Joe, and he worked as an electrician. He had been killed in an accident at work. That was all Mark knew of him, other than his mother had always told them that he had been a very prayerful and faithful man.

A voice came from the hall, interrupting his thoughts, "Father?"

Father Mark turned around to look at the doorway where his housekeeper stood, drying her hands with a towel, with her familiar blue apron still fastened about her. "Yes?" he asked.

"Breakfast is ready, Father."

"Oh, good. Thank you, Joan."

"I've made up a sandwich plate in the fridge, and your dinner too. It will just have to be heated up. I'll be back Wednesday, Father. Are you sure you'll be all right?"

Father Mark laughed, "I'll be fine, Joan. Enjoy your visit to St. Cloud and tell your daughter I wish her a Happy New Year."

"Thank you, Father, and Happy New Year to you," she said as she took off her apron and went back into the kitchen.

Father Mark listened as she picked up her keys and went down the stairs. Moments later, the door opened, then closed. He heard her car start and pull away, and then the quiet returned.

The clock ticked as if it had been slowed by the genuine dread he felt for the coming day. He had felt very alone this last year. His sister, who was his best friend, had died. She was the only one left of his family. She was the one who kept an eye on him and would call several times a week. She lived in Wausau, Wisconsin, so he did not see her as often as he wanted to, but still, she was only a few hours drive at any time, and they would visit several times a year. But she was gone now, having died suddenly from a heart attack. He had offered Masses for her since, and many prayers.

He knew from his faith that she was okay, that she was in Heaven because if anyone deserved Heaven, she did. She was kind, loving to her husband and two children, and a joy to all who surrounded her life, especially to him. But though she was okay, and with God, he missed her terribly.

The clock ticking continued to fill the silence, and he sighed. He had never really noticed how loud it was until lately. He got up and went into the dining room, where a plate of scrambled eggs, sausage, toast, juice, and coffee waited. He sat down, said a prayer of thanksgiving, and ate. Afterward, he glanced up at the clock. It was only 9:15 in the morning, and he dreaded this because he knew another long and lonely day lay before him.

There was a knock at the door. He smiled and went over, peering out the curtain that covered the small glass window in the large oak door. It was Mary Smith, one of his long-time parishioners. She was holding something in her hands.

He opened the door, "Good morning, Mary," he said, more glad to see her than she knew.

"Good morning, Father Mark. Happy New Year."

"Thank you, Mary. Will you come in? I have a pot of coffee brewing."

"Oh, I'm sorry, Father. We are on our way to see my family on the East Side. but I brought you a plate of cookies."

Father Mark smiled and looked down at the carefully wrapped plate. "Oh, that's very nice of you, Mary. Thank you," he said as he propped the door with his foot and accepted it.

"Well, have a nice day, Father."

He nodded, trying to hide the disappointment he felt. No one took time for him anymore, it seemed. Everyone was in a hurry, but still, he was grateful she had thought of him. There were 400 families in his parish. Yet, she was the only one who was standing before him, wishing him a Happy New Year. "You have a wonderful day, too, Mary… and be safe."

"I will, Father Mark. Goodbye."

He watched her walk down the sidewalk, then closed the door and sighed.

The old days, when parishes were alive with people and visitors, were long gone. There were large parishes in those days, filled with hundreds of families, many having four, or five, or even eight children. There was never a dull moment around any parish grounds. Inside the rectories, too, there were usually three or four priests living in residence, along with daily help from secretaries, housekeepers, and the women who did the shopping and cooking. It was all so very alive, a community filled with joy, serving the needs of God's people.

Now at the age of 63, he found himself utterly alone in a large old rectory, seemingly forgotten by the very people he served.

Father Mark went to the upstairs front parlor. It looked out through narrow windows onto the silent commercial street below. His parish was in the middle of a thriving suburb with a large modern shopping mall. Normally this street was teeming with cars, bicycles and trucks, but since today was the holiday, it was quiet. Normally he would see could see the rush of people a shopping town naturally possessed. This year it only served, though, to remind him of the great disparity between it and his life.

At mid-morning, he took out his prayer book and slowly recited aloud his prayers. They were spoken slowly today, with a heavy heart, and he knew he was sinking. He finished and went to the kitchen to get some coffee.

The phone rang.

His first thought was to not answer because it was probably just someone who wanted general information on Mass times, which the answering machine would tell them. But in the back of his mind, though, he realized it was late morning on a holiday, hardly a time when people would be calling for general information. Someone might very well need his help, and helping others was his duty. This was the life he signed up for, the life he had always loved.

He quickly went over and answered the phone.

"Hello, St. Richard's."

"Is this Father Mark?"

"Yes, it is Father Mark. How can I help you?"

"This is Kathy Perusek, Father. I know this may be short notice, but my daughter and I were just driving by, and we saw the empty parking lot, and... well, we thought of you. Would you be able to come for dinner today?"

The words hit him hard, almost taking the wind out of him. He stumbled at the start of his reply. Inside, he felt overwhelmed, and he didn't know why. His eyes watered, and he cleared his throat, starting again. "That is very kind of you, Kathy. I... have... I mean, my housekeeper made me dinner for later. I am not sure that..."

"Oh, now Father, that can keep for tomorrow. We want you to join us. Can we pick you up at 3?"

A wide smile came over Father Mark's face. "Why, sure you can. I'll be ready."

"Oh, that's great, Father. We can't wait to see you."

Father Mark desperately tried not to choke up as he thanked her and hung up. But as soon as the phone was put down, he sat down and with his eyes watering up. They were quiet tears of gratitude. God had heard the cries of his heart, and he felt renewed hope, not only for Christmas, but for the year ahead as well.

* * * *

Barbara turned to Rosie, annoyed, and asked, "What does this have to do with me? I don't understand?"

Rosie asked, "Did you realize what some priests and ministers go through at this time of year?"

"No," she said defensively.

Rosie said, "There are many people who are alone during many times of the year that no one ever thinks of. Do you know the name of the Pastor at your Church?"

Barbara hesitated, then lowered her glance, replying, "No… no, I don't." Another tinge of shame landed in the pit of her stomach. She regretted not ever bothering to know such a simple thing. How could she, she never even went to Church. Her parents and grandparents had known the priests of their parishes well, even having them over for dinner from time to time.

Rosie paused this time, as if she was pleased, she had gotten through. She raised her hand into the air, and they were back in her family room before Barbara's Christmas tree.

Rosie pointed; Barbara bent down to pick up the next gift. As she opened it, the room began to spin, and she closed her eyes tightly and took hold of Rosie's arm. The date and place flashed through her thoughts.

January 2nd 34 A.D.
Bethany, Judea
The Ninth Day of Christmas

Barbara and Rosie were standing in the middle of a dusty road that smelled of the desert. Everything felt hot; she could taste the heat in her quickly drying mouth. *Was this what Hell might be like? Was Rosie showing her a glimpse of where she would be going?*

It was dusk, and there were no lights, only small fires burning inside some of the small homes that looked more like tiny stables. Rosie pointed to one, and in an instant, they found themselves standing in a small one-room home.

* * * *

Aaron came in from the cold with more wood for the fireplace. His wife Miriam was sitting next to the dwindling fire, waiting. She turned to him with her dark eyes shining in the firelight and a warm smile on her face, saying, "Aaron, the children are waiting upstairs. They want to hear the story again."

Aaron chuckled, "Oh, those little lambs of ours. How many times do they want to hear it?"

"Well, in fairness to them, you only tell them the story during the time of the year when we remember his birth."

"I know. I am happy to tell it as many times as I can." He stooped and put another log into the fire, then kissed her. "I will be down soon."

He climbed up the wide ladder to the upstairs loft where his family slept. He and his wife slept at one end, and his three children, ages 3, 5, and 7, slept at the other end. He walked into the midst of his children's collective greetings, keeping his head low so as not to bump it on the beams of the roof. "Good night, my children," he said, playing the game they always played.

"No, Papa," cried his daughter, Ruth, the oldest, who had been named after his mother, who had passed away many years earlier.

"Tell us the story of the Little Drummer Boy," said Tobias, his middle child.

"Yes," followed Abigail, his youngest and most tender child.

"All right. All right. I will tell you the story again, but only because it is the time of year when it really happened."

Aaron sat down on a stool next to their beds, then remembered he needed his prop, the one he kept just for this purpose. He raised his finger, "Just a minute." He went to the other side of the loft and took out a small drum made of wood and cow leather. His father had fashioned it for him before his death over 30 years earlier. Next to it were the two wooden drumsticks.

He carried it over, sat down on a small stool in the middle of his three children's beds, and looked into each of their eyes. He had told them the story only a few days earlier, just as he had done every year at this time. Once the season of the birth of Jesus had passed, he would tell them other stories for the rest of the year.

He scanned their eyes, putting on a serious face, then began, "Long ago, there was a small boy named Aaron. His father had fashioned a drum for him, just like this one." He held it up and showed it around for his children to all see. They all stared in amazement. Aaron continued, "The little boy practiced every day, and he became very good at playing his drum. He also discovered that he had a rare talent. Do you know what that talent was?"

Tobias smiled, "Tell us, Papa."

Aaron playfully widened his eyes and said in a mysterious voice, "When the little boy played his drum, any animals around him would start to dance."

Abigail blurted out, "I want to see animals dance, Papa."

Aaron turned to her, with his eyes wide, "And you shall, my little Abigail. Now, listen with your mind, and picture my words as I tell them to you." He continued, "One terrible day, bandits came to steal from the boy's family. The boy was the first to hear them. Their sheep started bleating loudly, and the little boy looked out his window, and that was when he saw four evil men. All the men wore dark clothing and dark turbans. They were trying to steal the family's sheep, which the family needed to sustain themselves. The boy shouted out of the window, 'Stop, go away!' His father and mother heard his cry, and they ran outside to stop the men, but the men attacked them, and sadly, the boy's father and mother were both killed. The boy saw them die and then ran and hid under his bed. The next morning, relatives came to see what had happened. They buried the boy's parents and took the boy away to live with them."

Aaron paused as if he were done, and his children waited. Then Abigail said, "What happened then, Papa?"

"Oh, you want me to continue?" Aaron asked.

"Yes, Papa," Ruth said on behalf of the others.

"Oh, okay. Well," Aaron said, in a somber tone, "His relatives tried to make the boy happy, but children, a terrible thing happened to that little boy's heart. You see, because of what happened to his parents, he vowed to hate people, all people."

Aaron paused and raised his finger, "Children, you must always guard against hatred in your heart, for it is a terrible poison." He then smiled and sat up taller, continuing, "But God was not going to let this boy stay that way, and this is where our story takes a turn. One day, the boy decided he could not live with people anymore. He took his drum that his father gave him and his three pet animals, a sheep named Baba, a donkey named Samson, and a camel named Joshua. He set off across the desert of Judea alone."

Abigail asked, "Is that why we named our camel Joshua?"

Aaron laughed. She had asked him the same question a few nights earlier. He replied, with an animated look on his face. "Yes, that is exactly why we named our camel Joshua. It is why many people name their camels Joshua." He paused again then started, "One day, an evil man named Ben Haramed saw the boy playing his drum and saw the animals dancing. He kidnapped the boy and made him perform in his traveling show, earning lots of money. But the boy would not take any of the money.

"Then, one day, the traveling show noticed a caravan of kings in the desert. They told Ben Haramed that they were following a star. Ben Haramed tried to get them to pay him to see the little boy play and see his dancing animals, but the kings said 'no'. However, one of their camels died that night, and Ben Haramed secretly sold the little boy's camel, Joshua, to them for a large bag of gold. When the boy found out the next day, he ran away and followed the star the kings were also following, hoping he might find his camel again. But he journeyed for days without finding anyone until he came to Bethlehem."

"Is that where Jesus was born?" Abigail asked,

Aaron smiled, nodding, "Yes, my little one. That is where Jesus was born."

Aaron then continued, "The boy followed the star to the outskirts of the city. It was a cold night, and he walked along a road to a place where the bright star seemed to be hovering. It was right above a large cave that was used as a stable. Aaron walked a little closer, staying on the other side of the road. He noticed a group of shepherds gathered outside. Then, he saw the kings. They were inside the stable, kneeling in front of a woman and a man. There was little baby between them, in a manger. It seemed everyone was looking at the baby. And then, children, suddenly, Aaron saw his camel, Joshua."

"What he do, Papa?" asked the youngest?

Aaron smiled, "I will tell you. The little boy immediately ran toward the stable, shouting, 'Joshua!' But just as he crossed the road, a Roman soldier was racing down the dark road in a chariot. The chariot ran over Aaron's little lamb, Baba, almost killing him."

Aaron looked up, seeing the children's mesmerized faces. His children always grew quiet at this part of the story. He continued, "Aaron picked up his wounded lamb, and he cried. He then carried it over to the stable. He approached one of the kings who were near the cave entrance and asked, 'Can you heal my lamb?' The king looked down at the wounded lamb and frowned, replying, 'No, I am sorry. I am afraid your little lamb is dying.'

"'Please,' Aaron said with his face streaming with tears.

"The king then turned to look into the cave at the baby as if he had an idea. He turned back to Aaron and said, 'But perhaps, that little baby can. He is the King of all Kings.' The king pointed inside where the other kings and some shepherds were all standing and kneeling. Beyond them, near the back, was a warm fire, and a woman, and a man, with a small baby between them."

Aaron paused, then continued, "The boy took his wounded lamb and walked inside. He went right up to the front of the kings and shepherds. He carefully laid his lamb, Baba, in the straw in front of the woman and her baby. He then pulled out his drum and began to play softly. There were other animals inside the cave, and at the sound of his drum, they all began to dance. The woman, who was the baby's mother, looked at the little drummer boy, and she smiled. Then, the little boy looked into the baby's face, and in one moment, all the hatred he felt for people fell away. He continued playing, remembering his parents, then began to softly cry. Just then, one of the kings touched the boy's shoulder and said, 'Look, your lamb has been made whole.' Aaron dropped to his knees and scooped up Baba. He nodded in thanks to the woman, and then he turned, and bowed to the baby, then slowly backed out of the cave."

"What happened to the boy?" his son Tobias asked.

Aaron sat up straighter and began nodding, "Well, children. The boy told the kings about his camel, and they gave Joshua back to him. He then returned to his relatives and began to live life like his parents would have wanted. He became a carpenter. And… one day he met a beautiful girl, and they fell in love, and they lived happily ever after with their children."

"Sing us the song, Papa," said his oldest daughter Ruth.

Aaron took his drum and placed it in his lap, just like he had done long ago in that stable, on that cold night in Bethlehem. He would tell his children the rest of the story someday that he was the little boy in the story, but not now.

For now, they did not need to know, but he was glad to share this wonderful story with them at this time of the year, and he hoped they would tell the story, too, and pass it along to their children.

He began to gently beat his drum and sing.

Come they told me
Pa rum pum pum pum
A new born king to see
Pa rum pum pum pum
Our finest gifts we bring
Pa rum pum pum pum
To lay before the king
Pa rum pum pum pum,
Rum pum pum pum,
Rum pum pum pum
So to honor him
Pa rum pum pum pum
When we come

Little baby

Pa rum pum pum pum
I am a poor boy too
Pa rum pum pum pum
I have no gift to bring
Pa rum pum pum pum
That's fit to give our king
Pa rum pum pum pum,
Rum pum pum pum,
Rum pum pum pum

Shall I play for you
Pa rum pum pum pum
Mary nodded
Pa rum pum pum pum
The ox and lamb kept time
Pa rum pum pum pum
I played my drum for him
Pa rum pum pum pum
I played my best for him
Pa rum pum pum pum,
Rum pum pum pum,
Rum pum pum pum

Then he smiled at me
Pa rum pum pum pum
Me and my drum

Aaron wiped a tear from his eye, remembering the night as if it were yesterday. The song always brought him back, back to that cave, back to Mary, and Joseph, and Jesus.

Only he and his camel Joshua were left now, but Joshua was getting old, too old to do anything. But Aaron did not mind, for without him, none of this would have happened.

* * * *

Barbara stood silently next to Rosie, thinking. She asked, "The Little Drummer Boy was a real person?"

"Yes, he was. Every year, he told this wonderful story to his children and grandchildren, and he made them all promise that they too would tell their children and grandchildren. That is why we still remember the story."

Barbara sighed.

Rosie then said, "Barbara, you have young grandchildren. Imagine how fascinated they would have been had you told them some of the stories of Christmas."

"C'mon Rosie. You know most of these stories aren't true. Am I supposed to figure out which ones are real and which ones are not? Besides, what would it matter?" Barbara was trying to deflect the guilt she was feeling.

"It would matter," Rosie said. "It would mean much to them. It would help them to believe in the unseen world."

Rosie had hit another nerve. Barbara snapped, "Oh, am I in charge of helping them see the unseen world? Isn't that your job?"

"Why are you always mad, Barbara?"

"Mad? What are you talking about?"

"I am talking about your anger. Throughout your adult life you have always been mad about something. Is it because your father was mad all the time?"

Barbara gritted her teeth, "Leave him out of this! He had good reason to be angry. His employees were idiots!"

"Not really Barbara. He just used that as an excuse to be angry with them and with his family. Yes, as he grew older the anger within him eventually mellowed, but unfortunately, his anger became part of you. You took it on."

"Why shouldn't I be angry?" Barbara snapped angrily. "People don't do what they are supposed to!"

Rosie didn't flinch, showing little emotion, but Barbara could see she was disappointed. Barbara herself was surprised by her outburst. *Was Rosie right?*

Rosie lifted her arm, slowly this time.

In the next moment, they were standing before Barbara's Christmas tree. The tree seemed to be fading in luster now. There were only three gifts left to be unwrapped. Barbara felt a shiver run up her spine as she wondered what would happen after she opened the last one.

Rosie said, "Are you ready for the... " She paused. "Oh, Barbara, you have gotten me so upset I've lost track. Wait... let's see, 12 minus three... hold it, I have to add one back. Okay I have it. Are you ready for the lesson of the Tenth Day of Christmas?"

Barbara sighed. She wanted to say stop. She felt good about her chances. But... she realized if she backed out now, she would lose all leverage. Yes, she had learned some things, but she was not a criminal, or a murderer. Why was she being dragged through the mud like this?

She reluctantly picked up the next gift and unwrapped it. The room began to spin, and she grabbed Rosie's arm. The date and place appeared in her mind.

January 3rd 2015
Brooklyn, New York
The Tenth Day of Christmas

Barbara and Rosie were sitting in two folding chairs in the middle of a basement in a what looked like a run-down inner-city house. The beams and floor smelled damp, and boxes were piled four high in every direction. Barbara cringed at the thought of what might be lurking behind them. She pulled her feet close to the chair, lifting them slightly off the floor.

"Why are we here?"

"This is someone I held very dear. She is like someone you know, too."

"Who?"

"Just watch."

* * * *

Maria lay on her bed in the corner of her mother's basement, coughing loudly, trying to clear her throat. She had lived here for over a year now. The basement was packed with stuff she had brought from her house. Over 50 boxes were stacked three and four high in every place, leaving nothing but a path that led from the rickety staircase at the far end to the corner where Maria had set up her tiny living space.

Maria had moved in with her mother over a year ago because her mother was in failing health. But that was only half the story. Maria herself was in failing health. She had some disease she could not pronounce, at least that's what the doctors said. She wanted to believe they were wrong, but she was growing weaker and that was what they said would happen. Before all this, she had lived alone in her own house. She had never wanted to live alone, and she never imagined her life would come to this.

She remembered when everything suddenly changed. Her husband, Bobby, had sat her down and told her he was in love with someone else. The next day he moved out, and it sent her world reeling.

It was only a few weeks later, at her physician's office, when Dr. Pappas gave her the grim news.

"I am sorry, Maria, but you have an incurable disease."

"Well, what does that mean?"

"It means you will continue to grow weaker. Eventually... it will be too much for you."

She asked, "You mean it's going to kill me?"

Dr. Pappas nodded.

"Well, how long do I have?"

"It could be a year, or it could be three years. It's hard to tell right now."

Maria left the office and went to her car and cried. She never wanted to go through life alone, and here she was, by herself, facing something she never imagined having to face.

The first thing that had come to mind was her two sisters, who had died too young, both of them only in their early 40s. Both of them had died alone.

The thought of dying in her house alone frightened her more than anything else. So, she called her ailing mother and asked her if she could move in.

That was a year ago.

As she laid in bed in the corner of the basement, remembering it all, a few tears began rolling down her cheeks. Her life was not supposed to turn out like this. She was only 47. The ravages of her illness had left scars on her face that left her unwilling to see people that often. The scars were not that noticeable, as her natural beauty overcame them, but they were the only thing she saw when she looked in the mirror.

Maria was the youngest of five daughters, two of whom were already deceased. Their father had died when they were all under the age of 6 years old. She was only an infant at the time. He had been gunned down during a robbery one night while closing his inner-city store. Maria often thought about how those robbers ruined her family's life for what amounted to a small amount of money.

That was the beginning of the hard years, hard years that Maria had been part of since she was a baby.

Despite not having a father, she and her sisters had high hopes growing up. They were all beautiful Italian girls, proud of their family and proud of their heritage. In those days, all their aunts and uncles and cousins were around. The large family, all living close to one another, acted as a protective wall around them.

But, one by one, the families decided to leave the deteriorating city and move out to the suburbs. Within a few years, it was only Maria's mom living alone in the city with her five daughters. Their relatives begged them to move, but Maria's mom would not. She still ran her deceased husband's store, and while its days of prosperity were long gone, it was her way of holding on to his memory.

Though the larger family had moved away, they stayed close for years, visiting each other. The strong family ties kept on, but only on the special days of the year, like holidays or birthdays. The rest of the days, Maria and her sisters were alone in the city, with no father to protect them, and once they came of age, one by one, the wolves closed in to ravage their lives.

When Maria and her sisters were young, they felt invincible and thought the worsening neighborhood could not affect them; but now she understood that they had been at its mercy their whole life. They had been powerless against the gang-riddled inner-city neighborhood, and it had not been merciful to them at all.

Maria's only daughter had fared even worse. Tragically, she got involved with a gang and became addicted to drugs. She had recently finished a one-year stint in prison for doing something Maria still did not understand. Maria blamed herself for her daughter's plight.

She finished coughing, then picked up a cigarette and lit it. She got up and opened the tiny, dust-covered basement window, letting in the cold December air. Her mom had asked her not to smoke in the house, but she rarely felt good lately, feeling sick more than not, and it was too much of an effort to go outside and smoke. She stayed by the window when she did smoke, and in her mind, it was not causing any harm, as her mom could not smell it. She was largely confined to the main floor upstairs.

She finished her cigarette, extinguished it, and laid down on her bed, completely bored. The bells from the nearby Church began to ring. They were playing Christmas carols this time of year, carols Maria had heard them play her entire life. It only served to remind her how utterly alone she was.

Maria glanced at the calendar. She couldn't believe another Christmas had passed, and the realization of this saddened her. When she was younger, she imagined herself being married and having lots of children. She imagined herself in a beautiful kitchen, baking cookies and cooking all the festive Italian foods she had grown up with. But now, another year had gone by, and it was very apparent that those days would never be.

When she was growing up, Christmas was her favorite time of year. The days leading up to and following Christmas were fun and exciting, filled with visits with relatives, fine foods, and special events, including Church. Now, she didn't visit anyone, and she didn't go to Church, and over the past few years, no one had visited her either. Now it was nothing more than a time of year that dragged on.

The thing that bothered her the most lately, though, was her divorce.

She never wanted it.

It had been thrust on her, the most terrible surprise of her life, leaving her suddenly unloved. She still loved her husband and dreamed of the day he would come to his senses and return to her. But time was passing, and that dream was fading, and she felt like she was fading now too.

The phone rang.

She picked it up and looked at the number and made a face. It was her cousin Angela. She didn't feel like answering. She had not talked to Angela in a long time. The last time they talked, Angela wanted her to come over for dinner. Angela didn't realize that Maria couldn't visit. She didn't fit in, out there in the suburbs. Maria was ashamed of her life, ashamed she was divorced, ashamed she had never amounted to anything.

The ringing stopped.

Maria felt worse now, knowing she had ignored her kind cousin. Her cousin was one of the lucky ones who got out of the neighborhood into the suburbs early. She ended up going to college, meeting someone, and getting married. Things turned out for Angela like things were supposed to turn out. She and her husband had four children together, and they lived in a nice home in the suburbs. Her children were all doing well, all following the life most people in the suburbs followed. Maria was sure that Angela's home was elaborately decorated for Christmas and filled with delicious foods and Christmas cookies. She was also sure Angela was celebrating Christmas the way it was supposed to be celebrated, like they used to do in the old days.

The phone rang again.

It was Angela again. Maria hesitated, then answered, "Hello?"

"Maria, it's Angela. Merry Christmas."

"Merry Christmas to you," replied Maria.

"How is Lindy?" Angela asked.

Maria had no idea how her daughter was doing, and it was a deep sorrow for her. She had not heard from her in a very long time, but she answered anyway, "She is doing fine."

There was silence for a moment.

Maria then asked, "How are your children doing?"

"They are doing well, thankfully. They were here on Christmas day."

"Oh, that's nice."

"Hey, I wanted to pick you up and bring you over."

"When?" Maria asked. It was the first step in her bowing out.

"Tomorrow."

"Ummm, I don't think I can. I don't feel that great."

There was a pause.

Angela said, "Oh, okay. Are you sure?"

"Yes, I am sorry."

"Well, listen. I have a gift for you. Can I stop by later?"

Maria did not know how to decline. Angela had not visited in a long time, and not at all during the past year. Why now? Maria wanted to make an excuse, but it was still Christmastime. She replied, "Sure, what time do you want to come?"

"Is around 6, okay?"

"Sure. I'll see you then."

* * * *

That night, after dinner, Maria waited in her basement living space. Finally, she heard a noise upstairs. It was Angela greeting her mom. Moments later, Angela called from the top of the stairs, "Maria?"

"I'm down here."

Maria listened to Angela's footsteps come down the rickety stairs. "Maria?"

"Over here," Maria said, peeking out and waving for Angela to follow the pathway through the stacks of boxes to the back corner of the basement. Maria waited for her.

Angela made it and hugged her tightly, "Merry Christmas, Maria."

"Thank you. Merry Christmas to you." Maria turned, motioning for Angela to follow. She sat down on the couch next to the bed and signaled for Angela to sit in the adjoining chair.

Angela held out a small package. "I bought you a gift."

"But I didn't get you anything."

"Oh, that's okay."

Maria smiled. She took the gift and unwrapped it. It was a small perfume set. "Oh, I love this. Thank you."

"You are welcome, cousin." Angela said.

Maria admired the perfume, and sprayed some on her arm, smelled it, then dashed some on each side of her neck. "I like this."

Angela smiled, then asked, "Maria, how is your health?"

"To be honest, not good. They can't seem to tell me what is really wrong."

Angela nodded, not replying.

Maria pointed to her face, "These scars really upset me."

"Oh, you can hardly see them," Angela said, heartily.

"I can see them," Maria said, as a small tear escaped from her eye.

"What's wrong, Maria?"

"I don't know. It's just a lot, you know. Christmas. My daughter. I don't talk to her. My ex-husband is a real jerk. I am really sad about that."

Angela lowered her head. "I'm sorry."

Maria looked up, "It's really hard." She brushed away a few more tears rolling down her cheek.

Angela asked softly, "Would it be okay if we said a prayer together?"

Maria hesitated. She had not prayed in a long time, but she replied, "Sure."

Angela reached her hands out, and Maria grasped them. They closed their eyes, and Angela began to pray for Maria, her daughter, and all her needs. They finished saying together "Hail Mary, full of grace. The Lord is with thee, blessed art thou among women and blessed is the fruit of thy womb, Jesus. Holy Mary, Mother of God, pray for us sinners, now and at the hour of our death, Amen."

Angela paused, keeping a tight hold on Maria's hand. Maria tried to dry her tears, and when she couldn't she laughed, and they both laughed and hugged each other.

They talked a while longer, then Angela left. As Maria watched her leave, she was so glad that Angela had come to see her. It meant the world to her, to be remembered, to be listened to. There was a tinge of hope hanging in the air of the basement, and she was glad that it was Christmastime.

* * * *

Early the next morning, Maria was awakened by noise upstairs. Someone was talking to her mother. She heard the footsteps walking across the room and then heard the basement door open. A voice called out, "Mom?"

It was her daughter Lindy.

Maria quickly got up, dressing, and drying her welling-up tears at the same time, and said, "I'm down here."

* * * *

The scene faded slowly, and Rosie and Barbara stood in the basement's narrow pathway, looking over all the stuff. Rosie asked, "Did you learn anything, Barbara?"

Barbara's lips clenched, and she shook her head, "I see a person who is a hoarder. This place gives me the creeps. How do people live like this?"

Rosie paused, then looked into her eyes. "Does your cousin Lori and her suffering family come to mind?"

Barbara shot back, defensively, "Lori, what has she to do with me? We lived our own lives as we saw fit. She is not my problem."

Rosie said, "Lori's letter to you was cry for help, but you ignored it. At that moment, it became a problem for you. It is one of the many reasons you are about to face judgment."

A chill ran up Barbara's spine, raising the hairs on the back of her neck. *About to face judgment.* She kept her facial composure, assessing her position. She was… she now knew… guilty as charged… on all counts. But what about the jury, what about the judge, was there a way to sway them? Not in weakness. She had learned this long ago from her father. Negotiations had to come from strength. She launched into her argument, "No, Rosie. No. You cannot pin some distant cousin on me. No way. It would never stand up in court."

"In court? This is not a trial Barbara. Your life was the trial. The trial is… for all intents and purposes… over."

Barbara froze inside. *Over?* She calmly shook her head conveying she did not agree. Inwardly, she was very scared by what had just been said. Her heart began pounding in her chest, and she felt the moistness on her palms brush against her fingertips. Not until now had she felt trapped. She swallowed hard, trying not to show any of it.

Rosie raised her hand high, and they were back standing in Barbara's family room in front of the Christmas tree. There were only two gifts left. Barbara picked up the next gift. She opened it. A date and place flashed in her mind.

January 4ᵗʰ 1944
Ardenne Forest, Belgium
Ten Miles East of Bastogne
The Eleventh Day of Christmas

Barbara shivered, as she found Rosie and herself standing in a snow-covered field in the middle of a very dark winter night. She looked around at the vast trees surrounding the fields. She looked at Rosie, confused. Rose pointed into a nearby field, and said, "Over there, Barbara."

Barbara looked. There were holes she had not noticed dug into the field. Helmets were sticking up out of them.

* * * *

Private Leroy Boulton pulled out the envelope from his coat pocket. His frozen fingers struggled to grasp it. He cupped his hands together, blowing on them incessantly to warm them, then opened the letter and slid out the small, folded piece of construction paper with writing on it. He pulled out his penlight, and clicked it on, then began to read.

Dear Army Soldier,

I am a student at George Washington School in Buffalo. My teacher, Mrs. Ibos, said we could write to you. We are happy you are fighting for our freedom. We hope you will capture Mr. Hitler and put him in jail where he belongs.

Please come home soon.

Tina Coury
Fourth Grade

Boulton smiled, looking over the letter again along with the drawing made with simple lines and circles of a soldier holding a gun with the American Flag flying on a pole next to him. He wondered about the little girl who had taken time to send it to him. He looked up into the stars shining brightly on this moonless night and said, "God bless you, Tina Coury."

He tore off the bottom half of the paper and pulled a pencil stub out of the side pocket of his thick army jacket. But he dropped it. He quickly shined his light down at the snow and blood-covered floor of his fox hole. The blood from his leg wound had turned patches of the white snow red, making it hard to see where it had fallen. Finally, he spotted it and carefully reached down to pick it up.

He settled down carefully against the back of the hole in a position where he could write without pain. He then took another few minutes to begin blowing on his cupped hands to warm them again.

Finally, he started to write.

My Dearest Thelma,

I miss you more than words can say. I wanted to write you at Christmas but was unable. There has been a great battle here all along the front. Our unit was overrun by the Germans only 18 days ago. Many of the men from my company did not survive. One of my best friends since joining this unit,

KC Stevens, was killed. His real name was Kenyon Charles, but we called him KC. He was a star basketball player in New York before joining the army. He was tall and strong and invincible, but now, he is gone.

General Patton's army came to our rescue, and they turned the Germans back. I actually thought at that point, that the battle would be over, but it is not. We have been ordered to push the German line back. We are working our way in the bitter cold across snow-covered fields, making our way back to the front line we originally held at the start of the battle. There are dead bodies, both German and American, everywhere. It is a terrible sight to see death, frozen solid, for all eternity, it seems. It's funny, Thelma. There is no black or white here on the battlefields. We are all just men, trying to win the war, trying to get home to our loved ones.

I am in a foxhole right now, trying to keep warm for the night. I was shot in the calf two days ago. The bleeding has stopped, but I fear I may not survive if I do not get proper attention before long.

The only thing that I hold to is the thought of you and the fond memories we shared last Christmas together. Even out here, in the middle of a war, Christmas gives me hope. A few days ago, we heard Christmas music playing from the jeep that delivered us food. One of the men I know said the Feast of the Three Kings is coming. He promised us it would be a special night and that we should look forward to it. It is in two more nights, and I hope he is right.

I long to be with you, Thelma. I am glad we married and glad for the short time we spent loving each other before I shipped out. I love you with all my heart, and because of the love I have for you, I promise you I will come home soon.

With all my love, I say, Merry Christmas.

Leroy

Boulton folded the letter he had just written and put it in the envelope with the child's letter for safekeeping. He tucked it into his pocket, vowing to mail it as soon as his unit made contact with the main unit. Then, he looked up into the sky, staring at the bright North Star. He began to hum a tune that suddenly came to mind, quietly whispering the words to himself.

We Three Kings of Orient are…. Bearing gifts, we travel a far. Field and fountain moore and mountain, following yonder star. Ooohh, star of wonder, star of light, star of royal beauty bright. Westward leading, still proceeding, guide us to thy perfect light…

He felt peace humming the song, looking up at the stars, thinking about his life, wondering if he would make it home to Thelma where they would raise a family together. He wiped a tear from his eyes.

Suddenly, he heard the roar of the German artillery in the distance. Incoming 88s started whistling down from the sky, exploding and shaking the ground. He held his head down, shaking, praying, as the whistling grew closer and closer.

He vowed in his heart if he made it home, he would hold Thelma tight and never let her go.

* * * *

Barbara looked up at her Angel Rosie with tired eyes. For some reason, she was feeling exhausted. Growing apprehension at what was coming could not be staved off any longer. She shook her head and said in a feeble voice, "This absolutely has nothing to do with me."

"It may seem that way," Rosie said. "Don't you know any people who would love to receive a letter at Christmas. Soldiers, prisoners, elderly, even perhaps, some of your old friends."

Barbara said, in a pleading tone, "I don't have time for things like that. Besides, this does not apply to me. Look, let's just move on. I am ready for whatever is coming."

She waited, then looked up, puzzled. Rosie was not moving onto the next lesson.

Exasperated, Barbara asked with tired words, "Who was I supposed to write to? Who was I in charge of encouraging?"

Rosie raised her hand, and suddenly they were in a darkened living room of a small apartment.

"Where are we?" asked Barbara.

"This is Judy's apartment. She moved back to Cleveland long ago."

"Judy! My roommate from college?"

"Yes," Rosie said.

Barbara looked around the empty room, and asked, "Where is she?"

Rosie pointed to the bedroom. Barbara walked to the door and peered in. The room was dark and there was someone sound asleep under the covers. Barbara glanced at the clock. It was 11 in the morning. She turned to Rosie.

"She was always a bit lazy."

"She is not lazy, Barbara. She is depressed."

Barbara lifted her head back, staring at the ceiling. "And this is my fault, how?"

Rosie shook her head, disappointed, and turned, and started to raise her hand in the air.

"Wait!" Barbara said, her face bearing not only exhaustion but worry now. Her judgment was coming, and it was beginning to scare the hell out of her. She suddenly realized her hard stance would never work. Whatever was coming she was powerless to stop.

"Wait for what?" Rosie asked.

With her voice giving way her desperation, Barbara said, "I'm sorry. Yes, yes. I could have written to her… or… somehow stayed in touch."

Rosie sighed, and with a subtle nod, lifted her arm.

Suddenly they were in front of Barbara's Christmas tree again.

There was only one lone gift under the tree, a grim reminder of what was coming. Now Barbara wished there were more gifts, any number, any amount. Her judgment was nearing.

She looked at Rosie with worry in her eyes. "What is going to happen after I open the last gift?"

"It is not for us to know yet, Barbara."

"I don't want to open it," she said, frightened.

Rosie only nodded and gestured toward the gift.

Barbara's eyes suddenly narrowed, and she stepped back and said defiantly, "No, I will not open it."

Rosie did not answer but only pointed.

"No, I won't!" she exclaimed, taking another step away from the tree.

"You must open it, Barbara."

Barbara's eyes began to water, and she realized there was no way out. She slowly stepped forward toward the tree and fell to her knees, half crawling the final step. She picked up the last gift, fumbling to open it. The room began to spin and a date a place flashed into her mind.

January 5th 2018
North Olmsted, Ohio
The Twelfth Day of Christmas

Suddenly, they were in the living room of a modest suburban home. A hospital bed and two large recliners took up much of the living room.

"I don't know anyone like this," Barbara immediately snapped.

"Barbara, this is your last lesson. Watch carefully. You will see greatness, and you will understand why at the end."

"Greatness? What... why do... " It was all too much for her. She buried her face in her hands, shaking her head. "I want to go home... to wherever you send me.... Let's get on with it. I... don't need to see this."

Rosie put her hand on her shoulder. "Barbara, it is the last lesson. Stay with me and watch it."

"Do I have a choice?"

Rosie shrugged, and said, "Maybe... but not really. Just watch."

* * * *

Donna Mae had been up all night worried about the coming year. It was her 18th year on dialysis, but this year she felt herself failing in many ways. She was bound to a wheelchair or her medical recliner. She could stand and turn, with help, to get in and out of the wheelchair and in and out of bed, but it was getting harder, and she feared the day when she would not be able to do that. That would mean one thing: a nursing home.

When the long night of restlessness was over and the morning finally came, it was the day after New Years'. The holidays were over, and it was back to ordinary time. She lay quietly in the hospital bed downstairs in their living room, situated not far from her medical chair, waiting for PJ, her husband, to come down from what used to be her bedroom upstairs.

As was their routine, he would help her get the day started by assisting her in sitting up in bed and getting her a coffee cup while they waited for the morning home health aide to come. When PJ came down the steps, Donna looked up, trying to make eye contact, and said in a weak voice, "Good morning, my honey."

PJ smiled at her and kissed her, saying in this thick Irish accent, "Good morning, Mom." PJ had called her 'mom' for years because she was the kids' mom, and it was natural to call her that when the kids all lived with them. Now, of course, that they were grown and gone, Donna secretly wished he would call her by her name, Donna, just as she called him by his name, PJ. But 50 years of calling her 'mom' seemed to be stuck in his mind, so she left it alone.

The home health aide arrived, and she assisted Donna with getting out of bed and getting dressed, as was their morning ritual. Once she was up, the aide and PJ would help her stand, transfer her to the medical chair, and bring her a light breakfast.

Once she was settled, PJ sat in his recliner across from hers and turned on the TV, as he usually did, and they began watching the morning shows that they usually watched. It was a new year, and with it came worries, her worries about what the year might hold for her.

She felt antsy today.

She had an idea, and she needed to tell PJ, but she feared his reaction. So, she waited for the home health aide to leave.

As soon as the door closed, Donna turned to PJ and said, "I miss the days when we used to have parties here."

PJ replied right away in his thick accent, adding a slight shake of the head, which she fully expected, "I'm afraid those days are long gone, mom."

Donna frowned and looked back at the TV. A few moments later, she said, "Why do they have to be over? Why don't we have a party?"

"We can't have a party now, mom. There is no room. Where would we put anyone?"

"Oh, hell, there is plenty of room. I saw a show on Oprah yesterday where a celebrity had a party celebrating the Twelve Days of Christmas. She had everyone sing carols, and they ended up with the Twelve Days of Christmas song. Everyone was assigned one of the days, and each group had to sing their part. It looked like a lot of fun."

"How are we supposed to have a party here? Who is going to get the house ready?"

Donna glared at him and said curtly and confidently, "We are having a party. I've just decided. I will take care of everything." She was feeling her healthy old self coming back.

PJ rolled his eyes while Donna picked up the large button phone next to her medical chair. Her first call was to her daughter, Christine. "Christine, I am having a party here on Thursday night, January 5th. Can you come over a few hours early and help me get ready?"

"Party, for what?" replied Christine in a skeptical tone.

"For the Twelve Days of Christmas."

"The what?"

"The Twelve Days of Christmas!" Donna shouted, thinking if she yelled louder, her point would be understood. "Haven't you ever heard of the Twelve Days of Christmas?"

"Isn't that before Christmas?" Christine said, sounding confused.

"No, it's after Christmas. It starts on Christmas Day. It was on Oprah yesterday!"

"Mom," Christine said, sounding annoyed. "You realize that January 5th is in three days. Who is coming?"

Donna glanced over at PJ, who was pretending not to mind and pretending to be watching the television yet giving away his true feelings away by squirming uncomfortably in his chair. She smiled and replied to Christine proudly, "Everyone I can get a hold of." She watched PJ lift his head and subtly shake it.

Donna then called her other daughters, Bridget and Megan, and asked them, too, to come over early and help get the house ready. There was lots to do, and the party would be in three days.

The next call was to her sister, Roberta. Without introduction, she blurted out, "Hey, I'm having a party on Thursday night. I want you to bring Ron and come at 7."

"Why the hell would you have a party on Thursday?" replied Roberta, in a way only a sister could.

"Just get your ass over here," Donna shouted, in her commanding, humorous tone she and Roberta often traded.

Roberta started laughing, "Fine. We will be there. What can we bring?"

"Bring whatever you like, oh, and call Colleen, Ronnie, Doug, Eileen, Michael, and Brendan. I want all your kids here."

"Donna, are you crazy? How many people are you having?"

"As many as I can call. Now call them. I'll see you Thursday."

Donna could see PJ was squirming in his seat, getting more and more nervous with each phone call she made, but she kept going. Next, Donna called her niece, Margie.

"Hello?" came the sweet voice.

"Margie, this is Aunt Donna."

"Hi, Aunt Donna!" Margie said with excitement in her voice. Aunt Donna had been loved and feared by all her nieces and nephews for all of their lives. She made them laugh, called them to account, admonished them, and always gave both good and fun advice.

"Margie, I am having a party on the Twelfth Day of Christmas."

"Oh, when is that?" Margie asked, in the same confused tone Christine had had.

"January 5th."

"In three days?" Margie said, greatly surprised.

"Yes, aren't you listening? Now listen to me. I want you to call all your brothers and sisters. I want you and your husband and all the rest of you here at 7."

"But Aunt Donna, that's a Thursday night."

"Margie, I don't want to hear any excuses. Now you do as I say so your Aunt Donna doesn't get mad at you."

Donna could hear her laugh, "Okay, I will do it, Aunt Donna. I can't wait to see you. What can we bring?"

"Bring nothing. We will have plenty of food."

"Okay, Aunt Donna, I'll see you then.

Next, Donna said to PJ, "Call Mary, and Nancy, and Tony." These were PJ's sisters and brother.

PJ sat up in his recliner, protesting in his thick accent, "I'm *not* calling them."

"Fine," Donna said. "I'll take care of it." She continued calling them all, including her brothers, along with her friends and all her nieces and nephews. By the time she was finished, there was a large gathering of people about to descend on their home in the suburbs of Cleveland, Ohio.

When Thursday arrived, Christine showed up first, at 2 in the afternoon, to help get everything ready. Donna was not home from dialysis yet, and PJ was alone in the living room, sitting in his reclining chair, waiting for the phone call to go pick Donna up. Over the last seven or so years, ever since Donna lost her ability to walk, PJ had been taking her to and from dialysis three times a week. He and his son, Dan, had purchased a used van with a ramp, and everything was working well in this regard. The only problem was, over the last year or so, Donna would be exhausted on days after her dialysis. She had not considered this with her party planning.

"Hi Dad," Christine said as she walked in cheerfully, brushing her long brown hair over her shoulder. She was wearing white tennis shoes, jeans, and a floral blouse. In her hand, she carried a bag with a dress and shoes she would put on after getting the house ready. "Where's mom?"

"She's running late. They said they couldn't get her arm to stop bleeding."

Christine raised her eyes, "Well, that's not good."

PJ gestured toward the kitchen, "Over on the table, mom has a list of things she wants you to buy. Why don't you go to the store now, and we'll get that out of the way."

"All right, do you need help picking mom up from dialysis?"

"No, I've got it," PJ replied.

Christine turned and went into the kitchen. She picked up the list from the kitchen table.

It read

Go to Giant Eagle

4 pounds of Black Forest Ham, sliced thin

2 pounds of Salami, sliced thin

2 pounds of American Cheese, sliced thin

1 pound of Swiss Cheese, sliced thin

6 loaves of Orlando Bread

1 jar of Miracle Whip

3 Bags of Chips

2 Bags of Fritos

2 Sara Lee Coffee Cakes

4 Pepsi, 2 Sprite, 2 Ginger Ale

Go to Gas Station at Dover and Center Ridge

Get 4 large Lawson's Chip Dip

Christine came back into the living room and looked up at her dad, puzzled, saying, "This is a big list. How many people are coming?"

PJ shook his head, "A lot, and I'm worried mom will be too tired."

Christine noticed an arrow at the bottom of the list. She turned it over. Something was written on the back.

Go to Office Depot
Pick up an order at the copy center for Donna. Keep it closed and give it to me. Don't say anything to anyone else about what is in the bag. Just give it to me.

Christine smiled, wondering what strange item she would be picking up from Office Max for a party. But she did not question it. If Donna wanted something, there was a good reason.

"All right, I am going to go to the store," Christine said. PJ reached into his wallet and handed her the debit card, then she left.

An hour and a half later, Christine returned with her car full of food and drinks for the party. Her two sisters, Bea and Megan, were there, and shortly after, her two brothers, Bob and Dan, arrived. They all had been instructed to come early, and they knew better than to contest their mother's wishes.

Not long after, PJ and Donna pulled in the drive.

Ten minutes of unbuckling, unhooking, unlatching, and extending the ramp ensued until finally Donna was rolled down the ramp of the van and rolled up the ramp into the house. Her head was down, covered by a blanket to keep her warm, and she was partially asleep. They wheeled her across the living room to her medical recliner.

Christine came over and stood on one side while PJ stood on the other. PJ asked, "Mom, are you ready to get into your chair?"

She looked up, too tired to answer him, and nodded.

They helped her stand, then PJ pulled the wheelchair away, and they gingerly helped Donna turn her feet, one inch at a time until she was lined up, so she could fall back onto the raised medical chair.

"Oooh!" Donna cried as her bottom hit the chair.

"Are you okay, mom?" Christine asked.

Donna smiled, "Yes, did you go to the store?"

"Yeah, I got everything."

"Did you get the Lawson's chip dip?"

"I got everything on the list, mom. We have it all on trays already in the fridge, ready to go."

Donna asked, "Did you go to Office Depot?"

"Yes, I did," Christine said, smiling, as she pointed next to the chair. "It's right there."

Donna looked down, nodded, then smiled and reached up, touching Christine's cheek, "Thank you, my honey."

Just then, Megan came into the living room with a small sandwich and some chips on a plate, along with a small glass of juice. "Here, mom. Eat something and take a nap for a while. We will take care of everything."

"Thank you, Megan," Donna said as she accepted the plate and placed her juice on the table next to her chair. Donna then looked around and announced in her take-charge voice, the one she had fearlessly used for 20 years as the front-end manager of a large grocery store, "All right, listen up. Let's move that hospital bed against the wall. Megan, when people arrive, I want you to put their coats on the bed. We may as well use it for something. Dan and Bob go downstairs and bring up the folding chairs. We will need them placed all around the room. PJ, help Megan push that couch down to the corner to make more room. Oh, Christine, get the coffee pot ready, so we can turn it on when the party starts. Bea, run the vacuum after we move the bed and couch."

Everyone got to work. The party was in two hours.

At one point in the preparations, Donna nodded off, and PJ and the girls slowed their preparations to make sure they did not wake her.

Around 6:30 p.m., Christine gently woke her mom and told her it was time to get ready. She helped her brush her hair, put on some makeup and a new shirt.

Before long, the doorbell rang. It was mom's brother Kevin and his wife, Kathy. "Hello, and Happy New Year," Kevin said as he came in and kissed his sister. Immediately they began laughing about something.

Moments later, Tom McGinty and his wife, Laura, and two children arrived. "Hi Aunt Donna," he said with a hearty look on his face.

"Oh, Tommy, come over here so I can kiss you," Donna said.

Next came Mike Moran and his wife Cathy and their children Erin and Christian. Mike was one of Donna's favorites because he was always fun.

"Happy New Year!" He announced with a loud shout.

Everyone turned, smiling, some shouting back. He could not linger in the doorway long, though, as mom's oldest niece, Colleen, and her husband Frank were right behind him, pushing their way into the house.

Over the next 15 minutes, a steady stream of friends, relatives, nieces, and nephews all filed in. Christine turned on Christmas music, and within a half-hour, the house that had grown quiet over the last few years was alive, bursting at the seams, with people who had not seen each other in ages.

Everyone was having fun, laughing, talking loudly, eating sandwiches and snacks.

Donna was on top of the world, enjoying the party from her recliner. At 8 p.m., she looked around and called Christine over.

"What is it, mom?"

"Christine, count how many people are here."

Christine looked at her puzzled but stood up and glanced around the living room, then went into the kitchen and peaked into the family room. She returned, "There are about 60."

"60, hmmm…" Donna said, thinking. She reached into the bag by her chair and pulled out a pack of small yellow Post-it Notes. "Put a '1' on five of these. Then a '2' on five more. Then a '3' on five more. Go all the up to '12'. Do you understand?"

"Yeah, you want 60 sheets with 1's, 2's, etc., all the way up to 12 on them."

Donna's eyes widened. "Yes, then hand them out randomly along with one of these."

She pulled out a song sheet with lyrics in columns on two sides. There were five songs on the sheet. Rudolph the Red Nosed Reindeer, Silent Night, Up on the Housetop, Joy to the World, and finally, the Twelve Days of Christmas.

Christine looked at Donna, "What are the Post-it Notes for?"

"For the last song, the *Twelve Days of Christmas*. The 1's will sing the Partridge in a Pear Tree. The 2's will sing the Two French Hens part, etc., etc."

"Oh, I see. Mom, you're a genius."

Donna smiled, "Go, make the Post-it Notes and hand them out. Oh, one more thing. Make sure Mike Moran gets a number 5. Let me know when you are done."

When Christine had finished, she let her mom know. Donna watched everyone standing around, looking at the song sheets, looking at the Post-it Note, as if they had to check three or four times to know their number. She could see the growing apprehension in a lot of their faces. People did not sing Christmas Carols anymore. People didn't even sing anymore. The world, in Donna's mind, had grown too quiet. Christmas had grown too quiet.

Donna made the announcement. "All right, everybody, gather together with the people who have the same number. I want the 1's over here by the door. The 2's next to them, etc., all the way around the room. The 12's will be here in the hall, completing the circle." Donna began pointing as confusion and laughter, and a grand migration took over the entire house.

"What are we doing, Aunt Donna?" asked Margie with a wide smile on her face.

"What do you think we're doing? We are going to sing some Christmas Carols. Now be quiet and get ready to sing. We are starting at the top of the song sheet."

Tommy McGinty called out, "What are the numbers for, Aunt Donna?"

"You'll see in a while. Now, everyone, get your song sheet out. We are starting at the top."

Everyone began singing tentatively at first, but the house was alive with joy by the third or fourth verse of the first song. They sang three more songs and finally got to the final song on the sheet, *The Twelve Days of Christmas.*

Donna announced loudly, "Now listen, everyone. Each group has to sing one part of the song, based on their number on the Post-it."

Mike Moran asked, "So Aunt Donna, I am with the 5's. So, am I Five Golden Rings?"

"Yes, that's right, Michael," Donna said smiling, knowing he would do a great job with that all-important part, because of his loud voice.

Donna asked, "Okay, is everyone ready?"

Everyone nodded. Some were looking nervous again, as suddenly only small groups of 5 or 6 people would be singing at a time. Donna started, raising her hand for everyone to sing the first part.

"On the first day of Christmas, my true love gave to me…"

Silence followed, and the song fizzled.

Donna's eyes narrowed, and she turned, glaring at the group, "1's! It's your turn!"

Everyone laughed and looked at the five people in the 1's section. They were all nervously fumbling their song sheet and Post-it Note, looking down at the lyrics, realizing they had all missed their cue.

Donna said loudly in her commanding voice, "All right, let's start again."

"On the first day of Christmas, my true love gave to me…"

From the group of 1's came the weak and feeble cry, "A partridge in a pear tree,"

"Hold it!" Donna demanded as everyone erupted.

She glared at the 1's. "I need to *hear* you 1's." Everyone laughed even louder as the 1's sheepishly tried to gather their courage. Donna raised her finger, pointing around the room, "And that goes for the rest of you! Now, from the top."

"On the first day of Christmas, my true love gave to me…"

"A partridge in a pear tree," came the loud cry from the 1's, and Donna raised her eyes in approval, causing everyone to laugh. Donna raised her hand high, keeping everyone moving.

"On the second day of Christmas, my true love gave to me…"

The 2's shouted, "Two turtle doves…"

And the 1's started to falter. Donna glared, and they quickly found their line, belting out, "And a partridge in a pear tree!"

The laughter ensued, but Donna kept them moving, directing with her hand and her eyes. Now everyone was on board, and they all cried out: "On the third day of Christmas, my true love gave to me…"

Then, the 1's, 2's, and 3's perfectly continued the song, one group at a time.

And so they went, pausing for laughter each time Mike Moran and his song crew would shout loudly and slowly, "FIVE GOLDEN RINGS!"

Finally, they reached the 12's, and around the room, they all went in a whirlwind of joyful, heartfelt singing, from the 12's down to the 1's. Donna raised her hands and her voice, leading the entire house in the final verse. "And a partridge in a pear tree!"

The last line was sung with gusto by all and immediately followed by clapping and laughter. Everyone talked and raved at how much fun it had been, and they all knew they would do this again next year.

Barbara looked to Rosie, wondering what she was supposed to learn. But Rosie signaled to wait. Another date flashed in their mind. It was one year later.

One Year Later

Donna's niece Margie and her husband Scott rang the doorbell at the home down the street from Donna's. It was where her oldest son, Dan, and his wife lived. They were not the first to arrive, as the house was already filled with people.

Dan opened the door, "Hi Margie. Hi Scott. Merry Christmas and Happy New Year!"

Margie came in and hugged her cousin, kissing him on the cheek, "Merry Christmas, Danny."

She paused, "I sure miss your mom. I wish she could be here."

Dan lowered his head, "Yes, we all miss her, but… we are going to carry on what she started last year. Are you ready to sing?"

Margie smiled widely, "Yes, we are."

"Great, come on in."

The large home was filled with all the people from last year and more. It was January 5th, and they were holding their Twelve Days of Christmas Party, just like Donna had done the year before, in what had turned out to be her last Christmas Season.

* * * *

In the corner of the room, a tall male Angel stood quietly, observing the gathering with joy. Next to him stood Donna. She was no longer frail, no longer unable to walk, or lacking energy. She was young again and strong again. He turned to her, "Look at what you started, Donna."

TWELVE DAYS • 140

She smiled, "I am so glad they are carrying on. I wish I could be there to sing with them."

"Oh, it will still be fun to watch them. Hey, why don't you do this next year, in Heaven? You have plenty of family and friends to draw on."

Donna's eyes widened, "Yes, that is a great idea. Hey, we don't have to wait till next year."

"Well, it's kind of late now, Donna. It's already the Twelve Days of Christmas."

"So, what. We can do it tomorrow. It's the Feast of the Three Kings. It is as good a day as any."

"But… but Donna… where? Your house here in Heaven is not that large."

"Oh, I know. But your house is. Can we do it there?"

The Angel sighed, knowing he had suddenly been roped in. He smiled, "Sure, we can."

"All right," Donna said, "Here's what I need you to do…"

* * * *

The scene faded from view and Barbara and Rosie were standing alone in front of her Christmas tree. There were no more gifts. Barbara turned to Rosie waiting.

Rosie asked, "Did you learn anything?"

"Well, I admire Donna," Barbara said, surprised she had finally connected with one of the lessons. "She took charge, even of her Angel. She was… a real leader."

Rosie smiled, nodding. "Yes, she is. You have half of it right. Anything else?"

Barbara didn't know, and she was too nervous to ask, but she realized it might buy her some time. So, she asked, "What do you think I should have learned?"

Rosie spoke softly, realizing Barbara was on the right track for once. "Barbara, you are and always have been a leader. Like Donna, you were given special gifts. Imagine the thunderous joy that could have come from your home each year. Imagine the countless lives of friends and family, and even strangers you could have touched by your generous leadership."

Barbara wiped a tear from her eye and smiled. She felt honored that Rosie had said these things about her. She really could have done exactly what Donna had done. She could picture her children, smiling, singing, happy, surrounded by all her sisters, brothers, even cousins. It would have been so grand... but now it was too late. Another tear ran down her face, then another.

She looked to Rosie, who also had a small tear running down her cheek.

Suddenly, light descended onto Rosie's face, and she lifted her eyes as if receiving a message from above. The light left, and she somberly lowered her glance to the ground, her face bearing a terrible look of resignation.

Barbara's eyes widened, "Wait, what is happening?"

Rosie lifted her arm, slower this time, as if she did not want to lift it because it held something she did not want to be seen.

The End of It

Barbara suddenly found herself standing barefoot, wearing only a white gown made of rough material that felt scratchy on her skin. She was on a wet wooden deck in the midst of hundreds of strangers, all barefoot, all wearing the same white knee-length tunics.

There were men and women alike, shivering in the chilly night air, holding their arms close to their bodies, trying to stay warm. Many were quietly weeping, many staring blankly into nothingness, some outright sobbing.

She heard waves lapping against something. The floor moved, too, gently swaying along with whatever structure it was attached to. All around her was a dense mist that made seeing the person next to her difficult.

She heard a wave crash onto what could only be nearby rocks and realized she was on board a very large old wooden ship. She heard flapping and looked up to see enormous white sails that had been hidden from her view by the mist. Now she felt the ship moving faster forward and rocking more, too as if it were entering shallower waters. The sounds of waves crashing against the rocks on shore grew louder and more frequent. Soon, the vessel came to a loud grinding halt that thrust everyone forward a few steps. As they worked to regain their balance, the motion stopped, and the boat settled into the water, gently knocking against the dock.

The mist lifted, and a large wooden gangplank was lowered. A tall female Angel stood on the deck at the top of the gangplank, waving for all on board to make their way down. Barbara got in line and gradually made her way to the line formed at the top of the gangplank. When it was her turn, she stepped up onto the gangplank and nervously descended down the 10-foot-long board, step by step, until she reached the dock.

As soon she stepped onto the dock, she saw Rosie. She was way down the dock, waiting for her.

Barbara ran to her. "Oh, Rosie, I'm so glad to see you. I am so frightened." She looked up at the mist-covered hills before her and asked, "Where am I?"

Rosie nodded with a grim look on her face. "This is not an easy place to be in. You are right to be frightened, but… you have a chance for redemption here."

Rosie turned slowly and said, "Follow me."

They waited for all the others to pass, then waited a bit longer, then walked to the end of the dock. There was a wide stone staircase with 12 steps. It was covered with mist and wound its way up to where Barbara could not see.

Rosie took her by the hand, and they stepped up a few steps. Barbara pulled back, "No, Rosie, please. I want to go back to the ship. Please, take me back."

Rosie tightened her grip and turned, "You must come, Barbara."

"Oh, please, no."

"Come," Rosie said, pulling her arm softly, trying to nudge her up.

Barbara lowered her head and complied, walking to the top.

When they reached the top, there was the start of a 6-foot-wide path. The path was earthy and soft and seemed like it was made of mulch. It looked like it went on for miles as it wound its way through a long grassy field, rolling up and down hills toward the distant horizon.

As Barbara studied the never-ending path, the mist seemed to descend like a blanket, as if it had been waiting to descend, to obscure the path from her eyes once she had gotten the chance to see it.

Rosie grimly nodded, then spoke very slowly to be certain Barbara understood, "Down that path, 3 miles or so, there is a large white house. That is where you will serve your time of penance."

"No. No. I have to go back home. Please!" Barbara looked out into the mist, then back to Rosie, watching her reaction carefully.

"You have no choice."

"No! I have to go home," Barbara demanded.

"People who are not ready for Heaven are given a second chance here. I took you through the lessons of the Twelve Days of Christmas, and still, you really did not learn as we had hoped."

Barbara erupted in anger, not able to comprehend what she was saying, and exclaimed, "All this just because of Christmas! I don't get it. It's not fair!"

Rosie waited for her to stop, then said, "Some people are granted the gift of understanding Christmas before their death. But for those who do not, they have to go to this place. It is called the Land of Reform."

Rosie pointed out into the mist. "They can be here for many, long, and hard years, but every year, during the Twelve Days of Christmas, people who have truly changed their hearts are released from here and allowed to go to Heaven." She paused and said, "Goodbye, Barbara. I will see you next Christmas, and we will see what you have learned."

"Wait!" she pleaded with desperation, "What is so important about Christmas! Please tell me so I can understand?"

Rosie turned away, then stopped. No one, it seemed, understood Christmas. Barbara was a casualty of the modern age, as were so many. She turned back, wanting Barbara to understand, and said, "Barbara, Christmas is the most magical time of year, but most people have lost sight of it. It is important because the Twelve Days of Christmas are not really lessons of Christmas. They are the lessons of life. If a person is living their life well, then they will easily keep Christmas well."

Barbara stood dumbfounded, unable to offer any defense. She understood all of the lessons now. An aching pit formed in her stomach as she thought back to all the years of her life she had wasted.

She had not kept her life well.

Her mad rush and elaborate, fake staging of Christmas was just a reflection of her everyday life.

Rosie wiped a tear from her own eye, frowned, and started to turn away.

Barbara suddenly remembered Donna, telling her Angel what to do. She shouted, "Rosie stop!"

"What?" Rosie asked, turning back.

"You have to give me another chance. I am demanding it."

"Barbara, I have already told you way more than I have ever told anyone. You will have to figure it out. You are smart."

Rosie shook her head and turned, taking a few steps toward the staircase, but Barbara ran to her, tugging at her tunic. "Wait, Rosie! I deserve another chance. You know I do. Give me that chance!"

Rosie turned, saying, "I cannot give you another chance. It is not up to me."

"Yes! You can, Rosie. I know you can. You can ask for me!" Barbara said, pleading with all her might.

"It's too late."

"No! It not too late. Rosie, I need you to do this for me."

Rosie lowered her glance as another tear ran down her cheek. She turned and started to walk toward the staircase.

Suddenly dark storm clouds began gathering and swirling, and the wind kicked up in the darkening skies. Barbara fell to her knees, crying uncontrollably, pleading with folded hands, "Oh, please, Rosie, I beg you, please don't leave me here. Not in this fog. I understand, now, Rosie. I do. *I will keep Christmas well, and I will keep my life well! Oh please, Rosie, I will!*"

Barbara looked up, seeing Rosie turn and look up into the thick swirling clouds with worry on her face. Lightning flashed across the sky, and then, in a brief moment, a sliver of sun lit Rosie's face, but in the next moment, it was gone, and then, Rosie was gone, faded into the mist.

"No!" Barbara screamed, reaching out in vain, collapsing on the ground, weeping incessantly. "Please, please, I will change, please don't leave me here. I understand now. Please! Please!" She sobbed and sobbed, hoping and begging with all her heart.

Then, she laid down on the mulch path, curled up, and fell asleep, too tired to even cry a moment longer.

* * * *

Barbara's mind stirred, and she was too afraid, too weak to even try to open her heavy eyelids. She could see lights and an all-white room. She laid still for several moments, imagining herself in the large white house. She imagined the frightening mist all around her. A soft faint beeping sound came into focus. She sighed and exhaled loudly.

The beeping continued.

She heard a faint, familiar voice, "Mom! Mom!"

Barbara's brow furrowed, and she tried to listen.

"She's waking up! She's waking up!" the voice cried.

Barbara hesitantly opened her eyes halfway and saw the shadows of several people around her looking down at her. The beeps became louder, and she realized she was in a hospital. She opened her eyes fully and saw the faces of her two daughters and a nurse.

"Mom," her oldest daughter Laura said, beginning to cry.

Barbara tried to talk but was only able to muster an unintelligible whisper.

The medical team rushed in and began working on her. Her bed was slightly elevated, so she was in a half sitting position. She lifted her hand, signaling she wanted to write something. They brought her a pad and pen. Barbara slowly wrote, "What happened?"

"You have been a coma for five months."

Barbara smiled, closing her eyes, and began to cry. She was happier than she had ever been in her life.

An hour later, her husband Todd raced into the hospital room. Her heart leaped. She was ashamed of what she had turned their marriage into.

He ran to her side and bent down, kissing her. "Honey, I'm so glad you are okay."

Barbara choked back tears, and despite the pain in her throat, whispered, "I... I'm sorry. I... will change." She half-smiled as tears washed down her face, seeing in his eyes that he accepted her apology.

The entire day was filled with doctors, nurses, tests, and brief moments with her daughters and husband. Finally, and reluctantly, she fell asleep, thinking of Rosie.

Early the next morning, Barbara sat alone in her hospital room, gazing with wonder at the morning sun splashing across the wall of her room. She had rarely taken time in the past even to notice things like this. She glanced at her side table and noticed her phone. She picked up the phone and dialed.

"Hello?"

"Gwen?"

"Barbara! Barbara! You are awake! Oh, thanks be to God."

Barbara started to cry, "I love you, Gwen. I know you prayed for me."

"Yes, we did. Oh my God, I am so happy to hear your voice."

"Is... is Stephanie there?"

"Yes, she is in kitchen. Hold on."

Barbara listened as Gwen shouted, "Everyone come here, Aunt Barbara has woken up! She is on the phone. Stephanie! She wants to talk to you."

There was a pause.

"Hello?" Stephanie said.

Barbara cleared her throat and tried to calm the racing emotions she felt, "Stephanie, I want to say that I love you, and I am proud of you. I want to spend more time with you this year. Thank you for praying for me when I had my stroke."

"Oh, sure, Aunt Barbara. You're welcome. I would like to spend time with you, too."

"Okay, please know that I love you, and I will help you in any way I can. Please put your mom back on."

There was another pause.

Gwen got on. "Barbara?"

"Gwen, I have to go, but I will see you all soon. As soon as I get better, we are coming over to have some of Mom's famous pizza, and... if you don't mind, maybe we could sing some old songs."

"Sure, Barbara. You get better. We will talk soon."

"Okay, bye."

Barbara hung up and wiped the tears from her eyes. She looked up at the ceiling, so grateful for everything. She wondered if Rosie was watching her. She hoped so.

* * * *

The following week Barbara came home. She called her office and was updated on everything. Her husband Todd had stepped in and was working to hold her team together while she had been in the hospital.

She asked for Stan.

Moments later, Stan got on the phone. "Hello, Barbara. I am so glad you are okay."

Barbara could hear the nervousness in his voice, and she regretted causing it. She said in as kind of tone as she could, "Stan, thank you very much. I appreciate your saying that. I have a quick question. Did you ever finish calculating the Christmas bonuses?"

"I did, but then, well, you had your stroke."

"Okay, I want you to pay them out now. And make them 50 percent more. Do you understand?"

"Uhh, yes. Absolutely. I will do it right away."

"Put Jerry Tracek's bonus at the front desk in an envelope."

"But I did not include him in the calculation."

"Include him. He worked just as hard as everyone else."

"Okay, I will get it done."

Barbara wiped a tear away and said, "Thank you for all your hard work, Stan."

"You're welcome, Barbara. Get well soon."

She smiled. She could hear the sincerity in his voice. It was the first time one of her employees had really meant a comment like that. It meant the world to her.

"Thank you, Stan. Let me talk to Martha."

Stan transferred her to the front desk, and they transferred her to Martha.

"Hello, this is Martha."

"Martha, this is Barbara. I am sorry I have been such a jerk to you. I am increasing your pay effective immediately. I will need you to do a lot of running around for me, but I will make it very worth your while. And, you are not allowed to work anywhere, even close to holidays anymore! Is that understood?"

"Yes, I guess."

"Oh, don't worry. I will pay you for the holidays. You just don't have to work."

"Thank you, Barbara."

"You're welcome." Barbara let out a loud sigh of relief, then hung up.

She fell asleep, knowing there was one more important call to make for her business.

* * * *

When she finally woke up, she got herself some coffee. She sat by the front window, looking out at the beautiful day. She thought back to that fateful day and felt ashamed. She hesitated. She was afraid to face her prideful ways again. She picked up her phone, and looked up a number, then dialed.

The voice on the other end said, "Hello?"

Barbara was unsure of the voice, so she cleared her throat and whispered, "Is this Jerry Tracek."

"Yes, it is," he replied, "Who is this?"

"Barbara."

There was silence.

Barbara's eyes began to tear as she said, "I'm so sorry for what I did to you. I want you to come back to the firm. I want you to be in charge. I will be taking some time off, actually, lots of time off."

"I heard you were ill?"

"I was. But I am fine now. Jerry, I have just come to realize what a jerk I have been. Jerry, hear me out. I am going to pay you for all the time you were off work, and I am doubling your pay, effective immediately. Oh, and your Christmas bonus is waiting for you at the front desk."

Again, there was silence.

Barbara's heart sank. Was it too late to make amends?

Jerry said, "I have another job, Barbara, but I have to say, I appreciate your generous offer."

Barbara replied, "I want to make this right, Jerry. I am so sorry. Please come back."

Again, there was silence until Jerry said, "Okay. I will."

Barbara felt tears rolling down her eyes. They were tears of joy. "Start whenever you can, Jerry. Thank you. Call my secretary and let her know when you are starting so we can get your office all set up.

Oh, Jerry. Call Steve Garrity too and tell him you are on your way back and starting at the top."

Jerry laughed. "Thank you, Barbara."

"Thanks for giving me another chance, Jerry. I don't deserve it."

She hung up and sat there quietly, glancing out at the rising sun, deeply grateful for all that was happening.

* * * *

After a month of therapy, Barbara sat in her home, alone, reflecting on all that had happened. She picked up the phone and dialed the number Martha had located for her the day before.

"Hello?" came the muffled voice.

"Judy?"

"Yes... who... who is this?"

"It's Barbara, Judy. Your old roommate."

There was silence on the other end.

"How are you, Judy?"

"Ummm... I... I am okay, I guess."

"Well, I am sorry I have not been in touch. You came to mind recently. I want to pick you up for lunch, my treat."

"Oh, that would be nice," Judy said with a small lift in her voice.

"And I want you to plan on spending the day with me. I am taking you to my spa, where we are getting the works!"

"Oh, my. I don't know. Let me think."

There was quiet.

"I don't even have a bathing suit, Barbara."

"I won't hear a word about it. We will get you a suit on the way. I have everything covered. You just be ready."

"Thank you," Judy said in a feeble, quiet voice. Barbara heard a tinge of emotion too.

"All right, I will see you tomorrow, Judy. Oh, and Judy?"

"Yes?"

"I am sorry I did not stay in touch with you. But we are keeping in touch from now on! Got it?"

Judy laughed quietly, and Barbara heard her sniffle, then clear her throat. "I would like that."

"Great. See you tomorrow."

Barbara hung up. She had one more call to make to her brother Steve so she could find out about his son, Tom, and perhaps arrange a visit.

Seven Months Later

Barbara sat alone in her family room, looking at her Christmas tree. It was Christmas Eve. She glanced up at the clock.

They were late.

Finally, the doorbell rang, and she called out to Todd, "I will get it."

She opened the door, and her daughters, sons, and their families all began to arrive. "Merry Christmas," Barbara said, hugging them all warmly.

Barbara watched them all come in and observed with delight as they all began to notice the lack of gifts under the tree, as well as the normally elaborate dining room table set with some stacks of simple, plain dishes.

In a shocked tone, her oldest daughter asked, "Mom, where is everything? And where are all the gifts? And… where is Tia?"

Before Barbara could answer, the doorbell rang. "Tia has the week off. With pay! But just a minute, Laura. I will explain everything."

Barbara went to the door as everyone turned to see who it was. Barbara opened. It was Gwen and her family. Barbara could not help the tears welling up within her. "Merry Christmas, Gwen!" She said, embracing her faithful sister in a long heartfelt hug. One by one, Gwen's husband and all her children followed her into the house, all receiving warm hugs and greetings from Barbara.

Immediately, the fun greeting of cousins who had not seen each other in ages began. Barbara stood at the door, watching it all unfold. She announced, "We have one more person to come, and we will get started with some simple appetizers."

She looked out the front door window, scanning the street. Then she saw him, and she smiled. A tall man was exiting his car and turning to walk up the apron of the driveway. Barbara opened the door and yelled out, "Be careful, Father. It is a bit slippery." It was the priest from her Church, Father Jim.

As he walked in, Barbara said, "Merry Christmas, Father Jim." She took his coat.

"Merry Christmas to all of you," he said, standing in the doorway in his black pants, shirt, and collar.

Barbara said, "I am glad you can join us for dinner. And we will all be seeing you tomorrow at morning Mass." Barbara turned to the gathering and announced, "Everyone, please introduce yourself to Father Jim."

Her children all stared for a moment, not sure what to do. But Father Jim walked over to them all and began introducing himself to each of them. Within minutes the room was alive with life and the joy of Christmas.

Barbara's grandson came running from the family room, "Grandma! Grandma! Where are all the gifts? Why are there only 12?"

"Well, I will tell you all soon."

"Which one is mine?" he asked.

Barbara chuckled, noticing all the bewildered faces waiting for answers. "Oh, those are not gifts to opened tonight. They are... well... things we will be doing this Christmas Season. I warn you all. We are going to be busy the next 12 days. But don't worry, you can drop in and out as you like. I know you all have families and commitments. I encourage you though, to slow down and take the time as you are able. Trust me when I tell you, it makes a difference."

Everyone looked at her, puzzled.

"What do you mean, Mom?" Dawn asked.

Barbara laughed, looking up out the window into the night sky, hoping Rosie was watching. "You will understand in a little while. All right. First, everyone go grab a quick appetizer from the kitchen and come into the family room and sit down around the tree."

Barbara waited until everyone was in the crowded room, many spilling out into the dining room. She stood tall and positioned herself in front of the tree, holding in her hands the notes she had written earlier.

"Before we have dinner tonight…" she paused, suddenly feeling very emotional. Tears welled up in her eyes. She fumbled with her notes, and Laura came over and stood by here to help her, but Barbara gently waved her off. "It's okay, Laura. You can sit down. Just give me a moment."

Everyone waited, as Barbara stared at her notes, gathering her thoughts.

She looked up.

In the very back of the dining room, the Angel Rosie faded into view. With a smile on her face, she nodded, then waved goodbye, and disappeared.

Barbara's eyes watered even more, but she cleared her throat, and composed herself, smiling widely with the remnants of her tears still with her. She began, "Thank you for coming to our home, everyone. Merry Christmas to each of you. Now, I would like to tell you a story, a story of what happened to me, a story of the Twelve Days of Christmas."

The End?

No, it's only the beginning.

Taking a moment to post a review is a big help.

Review on Amazon

Sign Up for my Monthly Newsletter at dpconway.com

I promise not to annoy you.

D.P. Conway in Ireland

Copyright & Publication

Daylights Publishing
5498 Dorothy Drive Suite 3:16
Cleveland, OH 44070

www.dpconway.com
www.daylightspublishing.com

Cover: Colleen Conway Cooper
Contributing Story Editor: Colleen Conway Cooper
Developmental Editor: Caroline Knecht
Copy Editor: Connie Swenson
Final Proof: Marisa DiRuggiero-Conway
Beta Team: Books Go Social, Dublin Ireland

Made in the USA
Monee, IL
14 October 2021